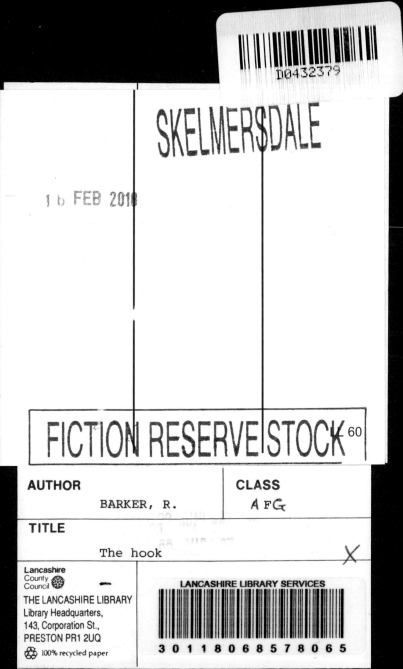

THE HOOK

COME AND TELL ME SOME LIES

THE HOOK

RAFFAELLA BARKER

BLOOMSBURY

06857806

First Published 1996

Bloomsbury Publishing Plc, 2 Soho Square, London W1V 6HB

A CIP catalogue record for this book is available
from the British Library

ISBN 0 7475 2749 0

Typeset by Hewer Text Composition Services, Edinburgh
Printed in Great Britain by Clays Ltd, St Ives plc

For Hugh

1

I gave up smoking when they read out the verdict. Well, not at the very moment that they read it out, because I was in the courtroom and you can't smoke in there anyway; but afterwards, when I went out of the door and knelt by the entrance to the cells. I cried and my hair swept the floor, drawing a tide of cigarette ash and a yellowed stub back and forth. That was what made me give up.

Everyone else thought I was giving up smoking as a gesture for Mick because he was giving up his liberty. Eighteen years. Longer than some people are married. Longer than the years you are at school. Longer than I knew my mother. Numbers pounded in my mind as I crouched hugging my knees on the dirty tiled floor.

I'll be thirty-nine when he comes out. No, that's wrong, they never serve the full sentence. He'll be out in twelve years. I'll be thirty-three, he'll be forty. I wonder if he will be bald.

Christy was in a night-club when she first saw Mick. Her sister Maisie took her there to celebrate her birthday. Spangles was loud and hot and the ultraviolet light made everyone look brown and healthy until they smiled. Then their teeth gleamed yellow. Christy was very conscious of this and kept her mouth shut, her lips folded like a seam across her teeth.

Mick had a long coat on and he was tall even though he was sitting on a stool. She noticed him when the strobing lights flashed across the dust and dog hairs on his coat. There were so many hairs that he was luminous. His back was turned, he leant forwards on the bar, the bright flow of his coat seeping up and stopping sharp where it met his hair. He had good hair, thick and nearly black, the kind that Christy's mother used to say was wasted on boys. It wasn't wasted on Mick. He turned round; maybe he felt her staring, wondering what sort of dog he had and if he knew how filthy his coat was.

'Christy Naylor, it's your birthday. You're twenty today.'
She didn't know who he was.
'How do you know my name?' She was flattered and dismayed, rushing with nerves in the noisy bar.
'I found it out.' He smiled and his teeth didn't gleam yellow. He came closer, his eyes never leaving her face.

She liked his eyes. She had drunk a whole bottle of champagne with Maisie before they came out and she was spiked with bravado.

'Do you want to come and dance?' Of course he would follow her; she moved towards the dance floor. Glancing back to ask his name she saw he wasn't behind her. He had stopped to talk to a man in a suit; he beckoned her over.

'Follow me, there's somewhere better I want to show you.'

2

His voice was low and he spoke slowly. He had an Irish accent and a scar like a frown on his forehead.

Christy followed him through a mirrored door beside the bar. They entered a small room with a carpet and dark walls. He closed the door and the silence was intense. In this room he loomed; the champagne bubbles inside her popped and she hesitated. She edged towards the door and felt for the handle through the gloom but as she turned it he spoke.

'Look, watch this, Christy.'

One of the walls slid back to reveal the dance floor. Maisie and her friends were bobbing in the crowd, their heads swinging like balls in time to music she could not hear.

'This is where the bouncers sit. They can see out, but no one can see in. They say they are looking out for trouble, but I think they're getting off on watching those girls dancing about.'

He stretched out his hand to her and he was so big in this room with his coat on that he seemed to be everywhere.

'What's your name?' Christy flattened herself against the farthest wall, afraid to be alone with this man and not know him.

He crouched by the invisible partition, his face white and carved from shadows, still among the frenzied dancers, out of place in his coat which folded like the wings of a sleeping bat under his arms.

'Mick Fleet is my name, and don't worry, Christy, I won't hurt you. I thought you might like to find yourself in here for a change, so come on and dance with me.' He got up and pulled a switch on the wall then led her to the middle of the room.

Loud music, the same as the muffled pulsing from the real dance floor, swelled in her head and they danced.

*   *   *

3

Christy was the second of Frank and Jessica Naylor's three children. Maisie was Frank's favourite because she was the eldest. Danny was Jessica's favourite because he was the youngest. This was how Christy saw it from the middle. She looked so like her mother that even Frank, who saw her every day, felt a shiver of loss if he glimpsed her unexpectedly.

Jessica hadn't had much hair left when she died; the treatment had thinned it to down as light as dandelions. Before her illness it had been a sweep of silver blonde like Christy's but not as long. Christy wore her hair loose and it flowed down to her waist. Her dark eyes, her light bones, her air of faint sorrow had all been inherited from Jessica. Even the way she stood at the kitchen sink, hands raw red, steaming, forgotten in the washing-up water as she gazed unseeing out of the kitchen window.

Christy felt she had been grown-up for ages when her mother died at dusk on her seventeenth birthday. The illness seemed to last for ever but in fact it only took six months for cancer to hound fragile Jessica to her grave. She wore a pink turban in the last weeks of her life, and Christy made them bury her in it. It gave her poor sucked-out face dignity.

Christy had a hangover the morning after her birthday. Mick telephoned her early. She was half asleep when Frank shouted at her bedroom door that she had a phone call, so when the voice down the humming line said, 'It's Mick,' she thought it was part of a dream. Her head thudded with the thickness of too many cigarettes and she was still dizzy and slow with sleep. Mick sounded buoyant and clean. He didn't smoke or drink, not even the champagne he had bought her at the bar. She groaned remembering she'd drunk the whole bottle herself.

'Why do you sound so far away?' Christy stood on one leg in the hall where the phone was, wondering if love or a hangover was slithering through her veins.

'I'm in London, well, nearly in London. I'll be back on Saturday. Can I take you out on Saturday night?'

A date. He wanted to take her on a proper date. She thought of eating marshmallows and chestnuts by a fire with him, even though it was May and the summer was almost here.

'Yes, I'd love that. Where shall we meet?'

'I'll pick you up at eight o'clock, if you like. See you then.'

The humming stopped and he was gone; Christy went on holding the phone, smiling and sweating in the hall with her nightdress on. Last night's make-up was sliding down her face and in the bathroom she decided it was as well that he couldn't see her.

Mick's car was black and new. When Frank led him into the house and offered him a drink Christy knew he was pleased. Normally he kept himself and his disapproval at a distance from her boyfriends. He didn't want to interfere but his eyes always said, 'This is wrong.' She hung around in her room fiddling with her hair, the door open so she could listen to Mick and Frank talking. The pleasure in Frank's voice rose like a speedometer's needle, gathering momentum as Mick explained that he didn't drink, had a job, liked fishing. Perhaps Mick did it deliberately, Christy couldn't tell if he was just humouring her father, but when she went in Frank was leaning by the fireplace rubbing the lenses in his spectacles, his face relaxed and benign.

Christy had forgotten what Mick looked like. Her memory blurred a face with film-star bland bones. But in the sitting room sat a stranger with a scar and a coat at whom her father gazed and smiled. He was more raw than she remembered, filling the floral armchair, his feet in the hearth. She kissed her father goodbye. Her limbs seemed strangely disconnected; she imagined them flailing out of control.

'Let's go.' She hardly looked at Mick.

Frank followed them out to the car, opening Christy's door for her and waving them off, still smiling.

Mick took her to a restaurant without asking her what she wanted to do. She liked that. They knew him there and they left him alone. Dark beams framed him opposite Christy, the candles made him glow and she was hypnotised by his voice. She floated above their dinner on a cloud of pink romance; Mick ate steak and onions, shovelling singed hunks into his mouth and talking at the same time. He was twenty-seven, he came from Dublin. He poured mustard from a plastic bottle over his plate and forked up three onion rings at once; Christy poked at her fish without eating it. It lay on her plate whole and unskinned, silver dancing in the candlelight. Looking down at it she thought it had as much chance of moving as she did held tight in the gaze of this stranger.

Mick was so hungry he was eating for her as well, and when he had finished every mouthful she felt full enough to burst. He was a freelance news reporter, the dog whose hairs still covered his coat was a lurcher named Hotspur and his car was a fuel-injection Ford escort. He talked right through three courses leaning across now and then to help himself to Christy's food as well. Christy ate nothing. His coat spread along the chair behind him and its black mass was part of him as he leaned forward over the table wiping up gravy with bread until his plate gleamed. Christy could hardly blink she was watching him so hard, impressed by the way he ordered wine without looking at the list even though he didn't drink and couldn't know what she would like. She felt tiny and iridescent, fluttering in front of this animal being. She hardly spoke until a moment when he was savouring the cheesecake and she was ignoring her sorbet.

'How did you get that scar?'

He traced his finger along the white vein and made his eyes cross.

'I had a lobotomy,' he whispered.

She believed him for a millionth of a second then he winked and they both laughed. Her drink slid off the table; icecubes bled into her lap but she hardly noticed.

Mick paid the bill to a sleepy waitress and he drove Christy home. She wondered if he would kiss her goodbye, and if her mouth would taste of fish and sorbet. His would taste of onions, but she thought she wouldn't mind. She wondered if he would stroke her hair and ask to see her again; she wondered so hard that she didn't speak until they reached the house. Then she rushed her words.

'You still haven't told me how you knew my name or where I lived or anything.'

He turned the engine off and took her hand.

'There's plenty of time, Christy. I'm not planning to go away, are you?' He said good-night and he didn't kiss her.

Christy was bitterly angry with her mother for dying on her birthday. Funny way to let go, she thought, when she took down the row of birthday cards propped among notes of condolence and ribbons from wreaths.

Her revenge was futile but she exacted it anyway. A week after Jessica's funeral she picked up a boy in a local pub. She chose the one her parents would most disapprove of if they'd seen him and she thought as she flashed her eyes at him and smiled: This is what I will do to make my dead mother wish she was alive. This is what I wouldn't do if she hadn't left me. Gary's jeans were grey with grease, his face smeared black with engine oil, and beneath the grime he leered.

When he had drunk a stack of pints with his friends, marking time with bum-and-tit jokes, Christy allowed him to drive her home. He stopped the car on an empty road and leaned towards her. She smelt alcohol and indigestion on his breath and turned away

'Come on, Christine, don't get stuck up on me.'

He couldn't even get her name right. Christy stared out of the window; black hedge loomed back at her. She was shocked by how stupid she had been. The sky pressed low; beyond the road on either side fields backed fields to nowhere. Far ahead an orange smear hung above Lynton and home. Gary's headlights arched a tunnel through the night, his hand slipped on to her thigh, rubbing a snail trail through her thin skirt.

'I'm sorry, I think I've made a mistake.' She tried to keep fear out of her voice, soothing him as she would a strange dog, avoiding fast movements or sharpness in her tone.

Gary took his hand away leaving her leg damp where he had touched it.

'You were leading me on in the pub, you wanted me then. You've got me now, haven't you? Just relax, girl.' The hand clamped back on her thigh, the other one rested on her shoulder and his wet mouth sucked at her neck, opening and closing like a dying fish.

Christy flinched, pushing him, pressing away towards the window.

'You frigid bitch,' he hissed.

Spittle scattered across the dashboard, tears dripped down

Christy's nose and into her mouth. Gary tried to turn her face towards his; she shuddered, her lungs filling up with fear. She yanked at the door and forced her way out of the car. He didn't follow her. Breathing sobs, she ran along the path of light from the car. She didn't dare look back, she wanted to go the other way, not to be within Gary's sight, but home was in front. Two miles in front. She threw herself beyond the reach of the headlights and doubled up beneath the hedge. Brambles scratched at her thighs and her hair caught on a twig but she didn't move while the car was still there, throbbing behind her on the road. Blood tickled on her legs and her breath came more slowly as she crouched in the wet dark, praying for Gary to go. Finally she heard the engine race and the car whined as he turned it round and drove off, careering fast away.

Frank was still up when she came in, sitting with slippers on by a dying fire. His expression when he saw her remained in her head long after she had forgotten Gary's face.

Maisie wanted to meet Mick. Frank had given an account of gilded perfection and she was incredulous.

'Christy? With someone like that? Come on, Dad, you're joking, aren't you?' Maisie shook back her hair and it settled like the curve of a fur collar, heavy and red on her shoulders.

Christy went to stay for the weekend in her flat in Lynton. Maisie had already moved out when Jessica died, and she didn't come back although Frank wanted her to.

'I'll have to be mother if I come home,' she said. 'And I don't want that role.'

Maisie's flat was on the third floor of a building near the hospital. It had four big rooms with rotting cornices and

9

ceilings mapped by cobwebs. The back windows looked out through dust to the cathedral spire and laundered grass folding down to the river. Maisie was engaged. Ben worked on the oil rigs so he was never there, but his motor bike was. From the kitchen Christy could see it in the middle of the sitting room, a pink T-shirt dangling from its throttle-lever like a lonely signal on a desert island. More clothes spilled across the floorboards towards it, twisted straps and sleeves flung out, bits of Maisie around Ben's bike.

They built the motor bike from scratch in Maisie's flat. It took two years, and when they carried the new tyres up all the flights of stairs and fitted them Ben brushed tears from his eyes and asked Maisie to marry him. They couldn't get the bike out now. Ben wrote every week and in each letter, after a few lines of Maisie-worship, he raved through page after flimsy page suggesting and vetoing ways of extracting the bike from the flat. His favourite was to ride it down the narrow stairs on their wedding day, with Maisie on the back in a white leather dress. Maisie thought not. She wasn't planning on white leather and anyway she liked the bike in the sitting room.

'It keeps me company,' she insisted.

Christy thought Maisie really liked it because it made her famous in Lynton. Everyone knew and admired her for doing something they would never contemplate themselves. Maisie needed admiration. Her hair was a beacon lit for attention, it fired her; restless and vital, she made Christy feel like a ghost, a version of Maisie lacking light, tired and slow in her flitting shadow.

Perched on the edge of the sink, her feet tapping, her fingers sliding through her hot hair, she pelted Christy with questions.

'How old is he? What does he do? Has he kissed you? How did he know your name in that club?'

Christy shook her head, ashamed of how little she knew, how little she had tried to know.

'You can ask him yourself. I'll phone him and ask him over if you like.'

Mick brought his camera. Maisie opened the door to him and the flash exploded in her face. Danny came up the stairs behind him and Mick spun round and caught him too. He put his hands up to guard himself, flinching, instinctively afraid of a looming stranger firing light at him. Mick laughed, Danny looked bewildered and edged past him into the room.

'Who's that crazy guy?' he whispered, hanging back with Christy as Maisie led Mick through to the sitting room, preening and pirouetting so he could see her profile.

'That's Mick, my boyfriend,' Christy hissed, irritated because Danny had thought Mick was to do with Maisie, not her.

Maisie brought beer from the fridge and they drank it out of cans. Mick drank Coke lounging on the sofa behind the motor bike and Christy could hardly see him. Next to him Danny rolled a cigarette thin and tight and cupped his hand to smoke it; his hair flopped across his forehead. Beside Mick he was fidgeting and fragile. Maisie paced around the motor bike, stretching her fingers to touch the leather seat, melting in reflection on the chrome petrol tank and exhaust. Apart from the sofa and the bike there was nothing in the room, no chairs, no carpet, nowhere to sit. Christy folded her arms and leaned in the door frame wondering if Mick would take her with him when he left.

'I can't believe you lot.' He was flirting with Maisie now as she draped herself low on the bike and played with the wing mirrors. 'You're all so beautiful.' He winked at Danny. 'You're all so different. Where did your parents have to go looking to get kids like you all?'

Danny grinned, liking him already. 'Lay it on with a trowel, it'll spread thicker that way.'

Mick laughed.

'What the hell, it's not often you get to pay a compliment to a worthy cause, is it now?'

Christy cringed at his corny smile, but Maisie played up. Mick took another picture and she posed, eyes wide in a face hard as porcelain, cheeks so hollow her beauty almost collapsed. Christy felt as if she had been tilted until all the tears inside her were poised to pour out and she backed away to the kitchen. How could she be loved when Maisie was there to be loved? Mick couldn't want her. The sink was full. Automatically she began to wash up, soothed by routine.

'You lucky thing. He's gorgeous. I wouldn't trust him an inch but I think he's dead sexy.' Maisie came in and opened the fridge for more beer.

Christy pretended to sneeze, lowering her head to peer into a greying saucepan, recoiling at the stench but not turning round. Looking into Maisie's washing up she began to shake with anger.

'God, you're a slag, Maisie. Sort your kitchen out before you start on other people's boyfriends.'

Maisie didn't listen.

'He's crazy about you. He's been banging on about you. I wish I'd seen him first.' She sighed, enjoying the thought.

Christy scrubbed her saucepan, teeth clenched, hating Maisie who she could hear laughing back in the sitting room.

Mick appeared in the doorway.

'Christy, are you ready? We need to get going.' He saw her smarting eyes and put his arm round her. He lifted her hair and whispered, 'I was scared of meeting your family. That's what I brought the camera for. It's my protection, you know.'

2

Frank was a contract manager in the frozen-food factory on the edge of Lynton when Jessica died. He had worked there for fifteen years and the ritual of his obligations shielded him from Jessica's ebbing life. He didn't believe his boss when he was called in a month after his wife had died.

'You can't make me redundant, I'm important here.' He heard himself from a long way off, the way Jessica told him she heard her thoughts when he sat with her in the evenings holding her leaf-light hands.

His boss's stomach dimpled behind a thin shirt.

'I'm sorry, Frank, I wish it was within my powers to prevent this.' The boss stood up, the stomach took a moment to go with him then sprang up his torso and wedged like set jelly above his belt. 'You will be missed, Frank, you will be missed.'

Frank started playing poker with a farmer outside Lynton. He didn't lose very much money, and anyway he had plenty now. The redundancy cheque was morphine to his grief and his wounded pride. He came back one night quite early. Christy was in her room sticking photographs of Jessica into an album she'd not had time to use. Frank walked in. His tie was slack, his wavy hair a blur about his head, and his eyes shone.

'I've won a field,' he said. 'Come and see.'

They drove in the dark to a waterlogged meadow and squelched across to look at the stream which ran like a vein down the side. Frank talked all the time, striding ahead through long grass. Christy floundered, her feet caught deep in the swamp. Her boot half came off and she toppled for a second before her toes found the warm tunnel of rubber again. Frank was shouting something up ahead and Christy pushed her fingers into her ears and stood still, feeling her life disappearing into a mire deeper than this field. After a moment she ran to catch up, desperate to stop Frank saying too much. She felt that every word he uttered as he paced over the meadow rooted his mad plan more firmly. He wanted to build a lake and a house and live in this field as a fish farmer. That was what Turndell his poker partner had intended, and the planning permission was already granted.

'It's a gift from God, Christy.'

'Dad, please stop it, you don't know anything about fish. I hate trout anyway, it always tastes of mud.' Christy grabbed his arm as he plunged into a ditch.

He was shouting now.

'Nonsense, we'd be mad to ignore this. It's a new start in nine acres of prime gravel. I'm going to negotiate with Turndell to buy another ten acres across there.' He gestured wildly into gloom.

Christy steered him back to the car and home. She couldn't make sense of his whirling ideas, but the mud-dank smell of the river lingered in her room as she fell asleep, pulling her down into dreams where she tangled with weeds and chains. The next morning Frank told Maisie and Danny and he put their neat little house on the market.

Time spiralled like the wind then. They lived out of

suitcases. Frank flourished, his energy recharged by every meeting where a builder scratched his head and said 'It'll be difficult to get that done' or 'There's no way round it'. Christy became a ghost, her voice sank to a whisper, the glow left her skin, now paper white with fine veins tracing lines across her brow and down her neck. Her hair lost its sheen and became a blob of yellowing cotton wool immobilised in a high ponytail on top of her head. She cried herself to sleep each night and woke with eyes puffed pink and glassy as the fish she loathed.

She wept all week, day as well as night, when they moved out of the patchwork suburb where she had lived all her life. Danny and Maisie stayed away as much as they could, hissing like affronted cats when they were forced to come and help, crackling the sad air of the little house. All its character was packed away in boxes leaving dusty rooms stripped of their dignity and forlorn, with smudges on the walls by light switches and worn paths across the carpets. In the end Christy did it all herself. She wrapped the pictures her mother had hung and the vases she had filled with flowers from her garden. She dug up Jessica's favourite roses and planted them in the mud-tracked field Frank called the new garden. There they sprawled, battered by wilder weather conditions than they had known in Lynton. She covered her childhood in layers of newspaper and packed it into cases. It would never come out again. Nothing was the same, not even the memory of her mother now the world she had built for her family was stacked in storage on the Lynton industrial estate.

They moved to a rented bungalow until the new house was built and the funnel-shaped field became a crater as the diggers excavated. The hole in the ground at the top of the field would be the main lake and out of it lorry-loads of gravel were pumped as fast as the newly exposed springs pulsed in. The gravel funded the lakes; mining it reminded Christy of the gold rush. Men everywhere, digging, rinsing tools, heaping yellow mounds of stone worth enough money to pay for the lake to be filled and even stocked a little. The money from their semi-detached house in Lynton was enough to start straight away on plans and materials for the new house on the lake. Everything was changing, there was no old life to hold on to now and Frank was so happy Christy couldn't look at him.

By autumn the first lake glimmered across the thin high end of Frank's field, a spine of turf separating it from the river. Lake Two was eating into feathered grass at the other end and next to it bricks heaped up into a house. Christy made Danny and Frank's breakfast in the bungalow a mile away each morning and sent them off to school and the fish farm with Tupperware boxes of sandwiches. She was meant to be starting at the sixth-form college in Lynton, but she was terrified. She knew she should go; Danny was managing his school, in fact he said he was glad to get away from the bungalow and the gathering threat of the fish farm.

On the first day of term she caught the little train into Lynton with him, oddly comforted by the journey through pale-gold fields of stubble littered with great cotton-reel bales. A distant village, its church towering grey above a frill of trees, caught her eye and she began to believe she might like living out in the country. The station they paused at had a platform stippled like shortbread and baskets of orange marigolds hanging from the pillars; low white fences bordered the car-park behind where a tangle of bicycles was hitched to a rack.

'This will be our station when we move,' she told Danny.

He grunted without raising his eyes from his homework.

They walked together up the swaying streets of Lynton Old Town past buildings with fronts overlapping, leaning down the hill drawing pedestrians with them. People always walked up the hill very slowly, not because it was steep but because they were moving against the flow of the streets, obstructing the downward trickle like a post caught upright in a stream. Danny said goodbye and went in the great arched gateway that led down towards the river and the cathedral and his school.

Christy continued alone through the shopping precinct and along the Market Square, a car-park until Thursday when the market was held. The college was beyond New Town and past the ugly plate glass and corroded steel buildings put up in the sixties to form the shopping heart of Lynton. New Town was a neat tartan of squares and roads lined with large trees which guarded prosperous Georgian and Victorian town houses. There had always been money to help Lynton grow, from the days of the wool trade, through light industry and now tourism; and every age was visible in the architecture propelling Lynton further along the river. The river Lyn was a black eel thrown on to streets which spread from the bridge in Old Town to the factories and housing estates beyond New Town. Christy had lived on the edge of this fantail all her life in an area where band-box thirties houses flicked in tiny streets to farmland beyond. Now she entered from the other end of town and walked through all the layers of prosperity. Lynton was small. She reached the college in a few minutes, her heart sinking as she pushed open the main door. It gaped black and wide in the flat concrete façade. She had enrolled the week before; now with slow steps she headed for her first art lesson.

All that week she attended every class on her timetable and cried for half of each session. The other students gave her rallying smiles but kept their distance; she was tainted by her grief, damaged and dangerous. They could not help her, it was best not to try. Christy continued to turn up for her classes, but every day when she entered the building she felt she had been swallowed and had become invisible. Only her art teacher noticed her and spoke to her by name. She liked him, his brow shone a path back across his scalp, hedged on either side by wisps of silver hair; his beard was pointed like a satyr's and when he was thinking he sucked the black leg of his spectacles as if it were a pipe. His name was Jack Hall.

After three weeks she had still produced no work and he asked her to come and have lunch with him. They arranged to meet at a table in the canteen. Christy was relieved she didn't have to queue up with him maintaining lively conversation while they ordered their liver and chips, fumbling cutlery on to the dirty trays. She arrived before him and sat down at the appointed table arranging her sandwich and glass of Coke in front of her. Her fingers twitched for a cigarette; she lit one, inhaling quick anxious puffs, and watched the door. He waved when he saw her and joined her presently with a cup of coffee. Jack Hall's smooth gestures and erect posture marked him out above the tables of swaybacked students shovelling food into their mouths or sticking great feet out from under the tables. His faded blue eyes were kind and Christy relaxed under his scrutiny. The confusion and sorrow she wore unconsciously behind every fleeting expression disturbed him here in the canteen among her carefree peers, and he looked down at his coffee cup so she shouldn't see his pity.

He offered her a cigarette and smiled.

'I'm worried about you, Christy.'

Tears perched sharp beneath her eyelids; she breathed deeply, determined they shouldn't spill over.

'You have taken on a lot at a difficult time. I wonder if you feel you are doing the right thing?'

She shook her head, unable to speak, the possibility of freedom rising in her, pulling her up from her slumped position in her chair.

'Do you want to be here, Christy?'

She shook her head; her hair flayed a bright hole in the ill-lit room.

'You've got a lot to deal with at the moment. Perhaps you should consider delaying your A levels until you feel more settled.'

Christy nodded, still mute, hoping no more was expected of her, thankfulness wrapping her like sleep, until every muscle slackened.

'I've spoken to your other tutors and they agree that you have great ability. We would like you back when you are ready.' Jack Hall sipped his coffee. 'I will write the necessary letters for you and when you feel you can come back, come and see me and I will arrange for you to take your place up again.'

'Thank you.' Christy flushed and smiled.

He changed the subject and began to talk about an exhibition he had seen at the Castle. Christy, dazed with relief, recovered herself and made him laugh with a description of her own visit to the show with Maisie who became paralysed in any museum or gallery after five minutes and had begged Christy to push her round in a wheelchair next time.

*　　*　　*

That evening she told Frank she was leaving college and he sank back in his chair, head in hands tight with remorse.

'I should have noticed, I should have made you leave, I should never have made you go, poor Chris. Why didn't you tell me? Your mother would have noticed, of course.'

'It's OK, Dad, I didn't know myself what the answer was until Mr Hall put it to me. I feel fine now, and I need a job.'

So Christy went to the fish farm with Frank every day and her plans for college sank under the churning disorder that was their future. The house was built but not finished. The rooms were all there, but like a cartoon waiting for animation, they needed colouring in before they lived or could be lived in. Frank designed everything himself, right down to where the bath would go.

Long and low and built of flint and reclaimed brick so it looked as though it belonged to the landscape, the house had three main rooms downstairs. The kitchen faced east towards Lake One and beyond it the road, invisible except in midwinter when the poplar trees along Frank's boundary wept their amber leaves and sent shivering branches high into the sky. Next to the kitchen the small study was Frank's favourite room, and he installed a fireplace across one wall and filled it with a wood-burning stove. With its doors closed, the stove squatted like a malevolent robot in the white room, but Frank was unperturbed. He planned to have his desk and chair right in front of the stove and thus to save a fortune on heating costs. This prospect delighted him. The sitting room had windows on three sides, casting slabs of sunlight and dust on to the wooden floor. Upstairs the bedrooms were tucked neatly above the study and the kitchen to give the sitting room all the height of the house and a ceiling of pitched beams like a barn. When furniture came in the great space swallowed it and gaped for more, but there was no more. Christy suggested a minstrels' gallery, but Frank laughed.

'Come on, girl, what would we do with a gallery? This is great.'

And in the end she agreed. The chimney breast crawled up one wall, a red-brick spine from which plastered walls planed out and away sending light and tranquillity down through the beams. Frank left Christy to decorate the bedrooms and took his fantasies outside.

His best moment was the day he ordered his island. Christy brought him coffee in the timber office perched on the edge of the field. They stared at paper edged by a shoelace outline of the second lake. Frank's pen darted at random to place a cross in the centre as if he were playing Where's the Ball. He gave the picture to the chief digger-driver and the next day his island began to bulge from the throat of the lake.

It made Christy laugh.

'God, it couldn't be less like Excalibur, could it, Dad?'

Frank scratched his head beneath the yellow building-site hat he had adopted.

'What are you talking about? This is a trout farm not a myth.'

She followed him as he began his daily walk round both the lakes and over to the new ten acres where digging was just beginning.

'You know, the silver sword rising from the glittering lake. We've just got a bump of mud sticking out of a few puddles.'

Frank never lost hope, even when the earth froze in January and Maisie came to the farm in her fluffy pink coat and freaked out. She said he had buried their mother's memory in ice and he was destroying the family; he sighed and patted her on the back and went into his hut to draw up more plans and forecasts.

A year later in the spring a tarpaulined lorry drove up, stacked with tanks of trout. Christy came out from the house and watched, expecting the fish to pour out in a gush of scales and water, but it wasn't like that. A man with a net raked through the tank and heaved a bundle of gasping bodies out and into the lake. They shone like stones in the shallows, tails fanning anger in ripples then gliding deep away. The breathless netting took all morning as two hundred ten-inch trout moved their thrashing mass into the lake. The lorry departed at lunchtime with casualties bobbing on the surface of each tank, their silver stomachs curving new moons in the blood-warm water.

The grass was a morass of mud; Frank sat in it, hunched and solid beside the shifting water. He gazed through his reflection.

'You put them all in, they swim around for a while and then you fish them out. I must be crazy.'

Christy crouched beside him and they peered at the surface, squinting at a mirror of sunlight glancing back at them, searching for shadows or the lone pout of a mouth rising for a fly. But the trout were invisible: shock waves had plunged them to the depths of the lake to flicker among mud worms and weed.

Danny was away at college now, Maisie had nearly finished her apprenticeship as a hairdresser and Christy had no proper job and no plans. College was impossible now she had spent eighteen months building this world with her father. Frank employed her officially, first as the money collector when people came to fish, then as delivery driver supplying local restaurants, and then as shopkeeper and stock controller. Each time his business grew another shoot, Christy tended it, and a year after the farm opened she did everything he did except catch fish and pay bills. She was second-in-command over two hundred fish, eight thousand babies (which she tried to call fry as in small fry, like the professionals), a tackle shop and smoke house. She was not quite twenty.

Mick loved telling people Christy was a fish farmer.

'I know what you'll be thinking of because it was my reaction as well.' He would lean forward to share a well-worn joke. 'She's not the fishwife type, is she?'

Maisie overheard him laughing with some friends at a club one night while Christy was at the bar.

'He's a bastard, Christy. What sort of creep laughs at his girlfriend's job?' Her hand in her hair stirred static. 'I bet he'd like to have you ironing his socks and cooking his dinner and not having a life, wouldn't he? You know what Mum thought of that kind of existence; if she had had more freedom she might not have got ill. All that pent-up frustration, Chris, and a man as slippery as your precious sardines. Be careful.'

Christy sipped the foam rucking on top of her beer glass.

'You know, they aren't sardines, they're trout. He doesn't mean it like that, Maisie; he's really quite impressed, I think. I'm taking him to see the lake tomorrow; he's been going on about it for days now.' She thought of her mother; she would have liked Mick, Christy was sure. Frank liked him, Maisie was jealous because Ben was unsatisfactory.

Maisie stretched haughty in her chair.

'You should watch out, Christy. There's something odd about him; you're getting in too deep too soon.'

Christy banged her glass down.

'Lay off, can't you. You just want to spoil it for me like you always do. You fancy him yourself. You admitted it when you met him.'

Beer draped a velvet pool on the table between them, sliding slow from an invisible fault line in the glass.

'Give me a break, Chris, I'm just trying to be sensible. You haven't got anyone else to talk to, you haven't got Mum now, you must listen.'

Christy swivelled her legs out and turned away. Maisie could clear it up, or it could stay there, she didn't care.

It was wet when Mick first came to the fish farm and Christy's boots slipped and creaked through the closeness of rain on warm grass.

'Trout love the rain. I don't know if they think it's the thud of something to eat, or if they just like the sensation, but they jump more when it rains.'

She led Mick to the edge and the surface shrank back from a rim of ink-soft mud before the next breath of water came in.

'It's not tide, it's more like an over-full bath. And the lake over there is for coarse fishing, bream and perch and pike and all that sort of thing.' She pulled Mick round. 'Come and look at the kinky clothes the fishermen wear. We only sell a few in the shop, but we've got loads of catalogues.'

Christy liked this sensation of being in charge with Mick. Usually he did all the talking and decided where they would go and when; he even ordered for her when they went to restaurants, and bought her drinks without asking what she wanted. The fish farm was her domain, Mick was less significant here than a maggot. She flicked her hair back and walked tall, proud of her efforts and her father's achievement.

Mick followed her into the office.

'This is a grand set-up, Christy, living off the fat of the land and all. You're one of the privileged, you know. D'you ever think about that?' He put down the filleting knife he'd been looking at and ran his hands through her hair, tilting her head back. Blue, nearly black, streaks of tiredness lay beneath his eyes; Christy saw her warped reflection stare back from his pupils. 'Privileged,' he murmured again, and his teeth were a fence in his mouth.

Christy stepped away talking fast.

'You can fish any time. There's no season for rainbow trout, only brown, and it started in April. I'll give you a card like all the members here have.' She picked up the filleting knife, her thumb juddering along the ice-thin blade.

Mick clasped her hands in his.

'Don't do that. You'll be cutting yourself and I'm liable to pass out if I see blood.' He was smiling now right back to his eyes, and Christy laughed over-long in relief. 'Will you come and fish with me at the weekend? Show me where the big ones hang around so I can be in one of those record-breaking photographs.' He gestured to a row of snapshots, each one featuring a fish like a massive eye held aloft by jubilant fishermen.

'I can't, I'll be working with Dad on Saturday.' She licked her thumb tasting salt and blood where the knife had nicked her. 'He can't manage on his own and on Sunday we usually go to Mum's grave.'

Mick whistled mock awe.

'You're a good girl, Christy. I can't lead you astray, can I?'

'This is my job, and Dad doesn't have anyone else now.' Christy heard the note of apology in her voice and stopped. Looking round for something to do, she opened the door of the freezer and began to count trout, her fingers sticking to ice-powdered skin as she stacked them.

She had told Mick about Jessica in a tight voice that hurtled out of her one night before he took her home. The moon warped green through the windscreen and she gazed ahead, keeping her profile to Mick. She could feel his eyes on her as she talked; he didn't touch her, he didn't move, he didn't speak until she had finished and was waiting small and worn-out in her seat.

'You can trust me,' was all he said.

Christy didn't know how long she spent leaning into the freezer rearranging fish barrelled like lead balloons. The rattle of the motor filled her head. In the bone-white gloom she reached deep into frost flakes for submerged fish, her arms chilling, each movement awkward. Finally she pushed herself back out into daylight and shut the door, skin flaring tight like blown glass in the warmth of the shop, ears humming as they thawed.

Mick hugged her, laughing.

'I've been trying to keep some kind of conversation going with your back while you were in there, and I thought it was getting somewhere, but you couldn't hear me, could you? I was asking if I could come to your mother's grave with you.'

She knocked over a pyramid of fishing stools by the door, confused and slowed with cold. There was too much of Mick in this cluttered shop, leaning over her, taking a step further into her life.

'Yes, if you like, you can come this Sunday. We always go late in the morning.'

A voice within her which she could not allow herself to recognise said: Thank God she's dead. She would like him, all right, but not for me, she couldn't bear me to have someone like him.

3

When she was a child Frank gave Christy things and Jessica took them away. Not always the same things, although there had been a rabbit, briefly. Frank brought it back from an auction as a present for the children. Christy knew it would be hers really because Danny was too small to look after it and Maisie didn't like animals, she liked Barbie and Ken. The rabbit only stayed a day, long enough for Christy to name it Felt and tell her friends at school.

When she came home, dropped off by a neighbour because it was Thursday and Jessica didn't do the school run, Felt had gone. Christy didn't like Thursday anyway. Jessica called it her day off. Usually she wasn't there when they came home and Mrs Edge the cleaning lady made them tea. Jessica would arrive while they were sitting at the kitchen table and she always went up to her bedroom and changed before saying hello to the children. This Thursday she was at home to meet them and Christy ran to hug her first before Maisie and Danny could reach her. But when Christy skipped into the garden to look at her rabbit, the hutch door was open and every sign of Felt had vanished. The hutch gaped dark and clean; Christy looked under it, shouting as she squatted.

'Mummy, quick. Where's Felt? The dogs will get him.'

She careered across the small lawn, stopping and turning, desperate to find him.

Jessica came out and knelt in front of her, holding her arms still for a moment.

'He's gone, darling. He had to go. We can't have a rabbit here. I've got enough to do.'

Christy stared at her mother in disbelief then pulled herself away. She ran to the hutch and bent over it sobbing. Danny pottered across to her and patted her with his small warm hands. Jessica tried to hug Christy and was met with brittle outrage.

'You can't possibly mind. You haven't had time to get fond of the rabbit. That's why I did it quickly. We couldn't keep it, not with the dogs and everything I have to do already. It would have been me who looked after it. It always is.'

Frank came home with a Peter Rabbit bowl to feed Felt from. He called Christy to take it out to her pet and when she told him the rabbit had gone he pinched the bridge of his nose hard and rubbed his eyes. Jessica sailed on through her day, bathing her children, cooking Frank's supper, pretending not to hear Christy crying in Frank's arms in the sitting room.

When Frank tried to talk to her she spun round taut and stinging as a whip.

'I'm not going to discuss the matter any further. The rabbit has gone. You should never have bought it without consulting me first and the sooner everyone stops thinking about it the better.' She sighed, smoothing her hands down the front of her dress, rubbing out the creases. 'There is no point in making this fuss.'

Christy could not bear to see her father plead with her mother and her mother ignore him. Frank marched back and forth in the hall, his face turning pink then purple with rage.

From a safe position behind the coat stand Christy watched him step purposefully into the kitchen and she hid her face for an explosion. None came.

Peering out again she could see Jessica over Frank's shoulder turn her wavering smile on him and reach out her hand to his cheek.

'Frank, please don't go on. You know I have enough to deal with without looking after a rabbit.'

Frank's arms stretched forward to her and Jessica walked into his embrace; Christy saw Jessica's fingers twining in her husband's hair and she knew Felt would not be back.

Mick and Christy visited the cemetery that Sunday and Christy was more nervous than she had been when Mick met her father. Jessica's anger at her illness caught Christy as if her mother was beside her talking in the rasping whisper she died with. She shivered. Jessica was in her head, hissing and venomous: 'You needn't think you can parade your handsome boyfriend here. This is my place, take him away.' Christy clutched Mick's hand, but she couldn't turn back, she had her flowers and the grave needed tending.

The cemetery lay between Lynton Hospital and the shoe factory, hemmed in and shaded so the grass was glass green all year. Railings twisted and bowed around the perimeter, unravelling between brick pillars and tangling with nettles and brambles in forgotten corners. Jessica's grave was near the hospital, too near when the sun shone and the tall shadow of the chimney swung across it like a pendulum. The chimney spewed smoke and Christy imagined hospital porters stoking an evil-smelling fire with spare limbs and organs.

Jessica was halfway down a row in a plot used so long ago that it was deemed empty again. On both sides headstones were spaced like neat teeth and for the first six months Jessica's grave was a gap in the perfect jaw, a hump of soil banked beneath turf squares until the ground settled and her milk-marble slab could be set. Christy wondered who the previous tenant had been, if Jessica would have liked them enough to spend eternity mingling with their remains. It had to be a woman: Jessica could not be buried with a man she didn't know, however much time separated them. Somewhere someone probably knew who had lain in this spot until they rotted to nothing more than the air tunnels of worms and the sandy soil around them, but Christy did not want to find out.

Today Jessica's spirit was malevolent, and Christy wouldn't have cared if there had been a murderer in the grave. Even as she had the thought, she could imagine her mother's mocking face, brows curving up at the ends in surprise: 'But you must know, love, they don't put murderers in Christian graveyards, do they?'

Mick waited at a distance from Jessica's plot, ignorant of Christy's internal battle, her desperate yearning for a sign from the grave, a sign that Jessica accepted her boyfriend, was happy for her. She stooped to lay her flowers on the ground; it was better to leave them strewn than to put them in a vase which the wind could empty in her absence.

Arranging them, crumbling last week's rose petals around them, she ran her hands across the turf and knocked her fingers on a stone. Pulling it up, she stared, astonished. A whole walnut lay on her palm, wrinkled and darker than the ones in supermarkets.

'Mick, look what I've found.'

He bent over her, his hand on her shoulder.

'Well now, you can take that as a sign from God, or if you are not so inclined, as a message from a devoted squirrel.'

She rose, laughing, and put the walnut in her pocket. The voice of Jessica's illness vanished leaving a blessing. She had never laughed by her mother's grave before.

Christy had vowed at Jessica's funeral that she would visit the cemetery every Sunday. For three years, unless she was away, she had done so, spurred by nagging fear that if she didn't go once she might never go again. She began to recognise other grave tenders, who like her brought their floral offerings at the same time every week. A pair of twins trailing plaits like thin tails down acid-bright backs made a noon pilgrimage to a plot three down from Jessica. In patent shoes their little feet pattered a rhythm along the paths and they looped arms near the grave, their coats a billow of neon yellow. The plaits were streaked grey, rouge smeared circles on four identical cheeks and Christy guessed the twins were fifty at least. The object of their fluorescent mourning lay beneath a black headstone engraved with ferns. 'Basil Shelton, R.I.P. February 14 1989.' He could have been their father; there was no clue beyond the ferns to his age or status. Perhaps he was brother or lover or husband. Ferns did not suggest romance; father was most likely; identical twins didn't share husbands, and these two looked like spinsters. Christy imagined them living together, brushing one another's hair a hundred times each morning and evening until it crackled and flew with static before binding it into tight pigtails.

Beyond them an old man crept towards his wife's grave, his skin bone tight, refined through the folds of old age into sheer antiquity. Each week he brought a posy from his garden and it took him longer than Christy was ever there for to bend down and place the flowers on the grave. She always smiled at him, even though his soft irises were blank, and her tears welled because his loneliness and dignity were so much more substantial than he was. He wanted to be dead like his wife.

The sun appeared for a moment from behind a cloud and rushed across the grass. Christy clasped her hands at the back of her neck, pulling her hair into a hood over her ears as the breeze snapped her dress against her legs and filled Mick's coat so it bulged across his back. They turned to walk out of the cemetery together; Christy in her shimmering dress with her hair flying leaned towards Mick. His coat embraced her, it covered her like a net catching a leaping fish.

Mick didn't take Christy to his house until their sixth date. She got drunk on their fifth date and cried at him the way hysterical women in films cry, all bosoms, teeth and sobs.

'You know me, you know about me, and I don't know you. You've met my family and seen my mother's grave and I've only met your dog.'

They were at a table outside a pub on the river and they had been there too long. Behind them the river lazed black and a pair of ducks snapped blunt beaks through a crisp packet. Mick was tense and unshaven, tapping his keys on the table, glancing at his watch, scratching in a manner Christy was convinced he had perfected to annoy her. He didn't answer or try to soothe her; she glared at him and her eyes smarted again. She marched off to the lavatory to wash her face and compose herself. All evening Mick had been buying her drinks, sighing because she asked for another straight away, and with every drink Christy slumped further from being able to talk to him.

When she returned a group of girls had settled on the edge of a nearby bench, their backs to the men on the other side of the table. The girls were passing photographs of a recent holiday between them, drumming their heels into the grass, shrieking like peacocks when an incriminating picture reached the top of the pile. Presently they rose and left, brushing out their skirts as they walked away, their summer prints a drift of coral and sea green above long brown legs. Mick watched them go, frowning, his fist a claw around his keys. Christy slewed her chin down on both hands, soft and uncoordinated, her eyes blurring into her hair which she kept rearranging further into chaos. She felt pink and fluffy and useless; she giggled, imagining herself as a giant Barbie doll, speechless and concupiscent, sitting there with Mick.

The ducks had gone and the river was slack and tired, its treacle surface broken by an occasional ripple. Mick hunched over the table, twisting his face away, his spine like a knife beneath his shirt. The silence between them stretched. She lit another cigarette, the last one in the packet.

Mick reached across and pulled it out of her mouth.

'You smoke too much, girl.' He crumpled the cigarette in his fist and scattered it, stinking and smouldering, on to the grass at their feet.

Christy's mouth gaped as the wires suspending her hysteria snapped.

'You're crazy. Didn't that hurt?'

Mick wouldn't look at her. His scar stood out across a fat vein and she stared at him, hairs creeping on her bare arms, willing him to look up and smile or take her hand. He didn't. He rose, stiff and taller than she thought he could be, and picked up the car keys.

'I'm tired. I've got to start early tomorrow, I'll take you home now.'

Christy sat small in the car, pressed down by silence. When she tried to say something Mick turned loud music on, bouncing his palms on the steering wheel, turning his car into a cube of sound too dense for Christy to penetrate. He didn't say goodbye when they reached her house. He paused long enough for her to get out then spun away before she could close the door, jerking down the track so the door cracked shut by itself. Christy didn't cry until she got to her room.

She thought that was it. She had blown it because she had been drunk. By Friday she had taken down the photograph Mick had given her and started wearing glasses again because her eyes were too cried out for contact lenses. She felt so ugly she was relishing it; Frank was sick of asking if she was all right and had gone fishing. Christy locked the office after work, balancing two plastic trays of mutant smoked prawns as she struggled with the keys. One batch of pink stumps slid to the ground and she stepped back on to them, grinding deformed commas into the gravel.

'Christy, you're killing the wildlife, or was it dead already?'

Mick was behind her. Before she could turn round he was hugging her and the rest of the prawns slithered between them and hung lewd and rosy on their clothes.

'These are for you. I've missed you, sweetheart.' He gave her a bunch of pink roses; they were a better colour than the prawns and their scent soared above the dried-out smell of bloodless fish. He had never called her sweetheart before.

She should have been cool and said she was busy, but he

disarmed her, whispering, 'You're beautiful,' which could never have been further from the truth than then.

Rushing to her bedroom to change she stood a moment in front of the mirror, her eye sockets puffed like ring doughnuts, the eyes themselves washed out and red-veined. Christy took off her glasses and threw them on to the dressing table. Her hair had separated into strings, dark at her scalp revealing grey glimpses of skin; brushing it was useless, it would lie dank and heavy down her back.

She yelled down the stairs, 'Mick, I've got to wash my hair. Will you wait?'

She put on a pink dress, giggling to herself in her bedroom, wondering if Mick would notice she was continuing the rose and prawn theme. He was taking her to his house tonight. She knew it even though he hadn't said so; and he was nervous. He had not told her much about where he lived and Christy preferred to guess than to ask. He drove fast, all the car windows open to dry her hair. They turned off the road and slowed to follow a tarmac track winding through pasture and woodland, neat fences dividing kempt cows from sheep and horses. It was so orderly it could have been a calendar photograph. It did not seem a likely place for Mick.

'The landlord lives up there.' He pointed to red chimneys scarcely visible in a cloud of trees. 'He's like something you'll find in a theme park, you know. He's got all the kit for his playground, garters or gaiters or whatever the hell you call them, and a shooting stick and a gun room. He got it all from vacuum-packed turkeys, poor sods.' Mick swung the car down a pot-holed lane through a tunnel of trees. 'I never thought I'd be getting this cottage, my accent's not right and the manager bloke didn't like me, but when I offered six months' rent in cash he handed the lease right over. He didn't even want to see my references.'

They were in a clearing now, stopping in front of Hansel and Gretel's house. Christy had never seen a picture of it, her childhood fairy-tale book had no illustrations, but Mick's cottage was the real-life version of the image she had always carried. The lopsided porch staggered under a rose blooming yellow, its branches roaming up and scratching at diamond-paned windows; the roof zig-zagged over the two little gables and was crowned by a twisted chimney. Christy had imagined that Mick would live somewhere macho, a tower block or an old warehouse or above a night-club. Even though he had said it was remote, even though there were no macho buildings in Lynton, she had never imagined it could be such a cliché of prettiness.

Mick sprang to open the door for her, faking courtliness with a bow as she went past him into the house.

'Welcome to Launderer's Cottage. It used to be called Laundry Cottage but I changed the name, it seemed more my sort of scene.'

The dog Hotspur lay flat before a dead fire thumping his tail but not moving until Mick called him. Newspapers and maps fanned across the table and a collage of photographs covered one wall. Staring everywhere, absorbing Mick's world, Christy was half curious, half afraid. Her other boyfriends had always lived at home with their parents in houses like her childhood home, or in bedsits in Lynton. Frank didn't like those ones. She had never been with a man to his own house before. Mick's belongings crowded the low room, books in swerving piles, records sliding out of their corner, pictures scattered on the mantelpiece and hung high on the wall where old nails gouged the plaster. Behind the door coats filled the log basket and trailed back into the passage towards another door. A sofa drooped in front of the fire and beside it a deep armchair. There was no other furniture save the table in the window. Hotspur bounced like a Yo-Yo at Mick's side, yapping delight; Christy was hardly breathing, unable to think of anything at all to say.

'I'd better feed this dog.' Mick went through into the kitchen.

Christy scanned the photographs, fast at first to see if there was one of her in his collection. She found herself at one end, pale and sulky in Maisie's flat; her arms were crossed and her mouth curved down at one end. She did not look glamorous or beautiful. But at least there was a picture of her. The others were landscapes, black-and-white and harsh. Christy didn't much like them, but she studied each one slowly, willing herself to be moved by the shadows cast on to lonely countryside.

Sounds of dog feeding clattered from the kitchen, Mick murmuring blandishments to Hotspur who whined a crescendo of hunger. The long evening light melted through the window, freckled where it had passed leaves silhouetted against the sun. Leaves and more leaves, nothing else for miles. Christy thought of the long track Mick had driven her down. Even the chimneys of the landlord's house were far away, back towards the road and the world. She was alone with Mick and his belongings. What was she supposed to do now?

She tried sitting down, perching on the edge of the sofa. The clatter of the dog's plate in the kitchen made her start and she jumped up again. Should she go and offer to help? No, Mick's backview filled the kitchen door. There was no room for her in there with him. She picked up a magazine and stared at the cover. She dropped it and picked up another one. Unable to keep still she walked around the room, one hand trailing the sofa back. She needed air. Relieved by a decision, she reached to open the back door beyond a muddle of coats. It was not the back door. A mop, a broom, golf clubs and an axe fell like spillikins into the room. Panicking now, she bent to pick them up, wedging them against curtain poles and fishing rods in the corner of the cupboard. She turned to go out of the front door.

Mick called through, 'Are you all right in there, Christy?'

And she managed to answer, 'Yes, fine, I'm just going to look at the garden.'

4

Jessica Naylor's coffin was smaller than Christy expected it to be. Although Jessica was a slight woman with narrow hands and movements as fluid as a Siamese cat's, Christy could only remember her as huge. The hole her mother left gaped, and from the childhood memories soaring through the first days of loss stared a monumental Jessica. Perhaps because I was little then, Christy thought, unable yet to form another thought: Perhaps I was afraid of her. The memories were dimly lit, but in them Jessica was lambent, her children strung around her like baubles on a bracelet.

When Christy was tiny Jessica bloomed youth; she would hold her daughter by the hand and stand, poised at the front door or outside a shop or in the playground, until someone animated her with a compliment, an admiring smile.

'How lovely to see such a beautiful mother and child,' the Vicar beamed, squeezing Christy's cheek with bone-cold fingers.

Christy hid her face in Jessica's neck, hugging her, breathing in her familiar scent of China tea and sunshine.

Jessica didn't push Christy away then. She kept the little house neat and clean. She was happy when Frank came home and the hall smelt of polish, the kitchen of dinner. If the children were in bed and asleep she shone with smooth accomplishment. Frank sat at the kitchen table with his tie undone, clean-cut in his suit among the frills of her frilly kitchen.

She chopped vegetables and told him about her day.

'We've cleaned out the goldfish today. Christy's one had some fungus on it but the pet shop gave me blue liquid to squirt into the water. The children loved that.'

She could do it, she really could. This small life Frank had brought her to was enough. She didn't want to run back to her parents and the big house where she grew up. She didn't need to be called Miss by men on the estate now that she had local shops where she was Mrs Naylor.

'Naylor. Such a ghastly name. What a pity.' Her mother's sole comment when Jessica told her parents she was getting married was still resonant in her mind, but she never told Frank. She loved him too much to hurt him like that.

Frank gave her everything he had promised. The house was small, but they weren't in debt, and Jessica could enjoy bringing up the children without bothering her head with bills and mortgages. She made picnics and cleaned the house while the girls were at school, laughing at herself when she started tying her hair in a coloured scarf to keep it off her face. Every day that her house and family were in order was a mark of proof that she had made the right choice. And that her parents were wrong. She was sure Frank would become something more than a factory manager and she sat often on the window seat dreaming of their future, of trips to London to the theatre and holidays abroad. In the meantime, Frank encouraged her to go to the hairdresser once a week and to buy a new dress twice a year. She loved the sparkle in his blue eyes when he looked at her and the strength in his narrow face. They were a handsome couple at church on Sundays, the three children playing around their pew, docile and pretty, never screaming or wiping noses on the backs of their hands.

The years rolled by punctuated by the small victories and losses of childhood. For Jessica nothing changed. She cleaned and cooked and welcomed Frank home every night, sending him to work with a clean shirt every morning. He didn't always ask how her day had been, and he read the paper now instead of listening when she told him. Alone in front of her mirror, she knew why. Her silver beauty was tarnished, her hair was fading. The mother-of-pearl skin had begun to tighten around her nose and sag along her jaw, not much yet, but she saw the traced lines of what was to come and spread her fingers across her face in horror. Looking through them she could see the reflection of the backs of her hands in the mirror, reddened knuckles and rings sliding where her plump flesh had hardened and shrunk.

Now when she looked at Christy her pride was eclipsed by jealousy. Christy's slender youth mocked her in a way that Maisie's never could. Maisie was a foil, a vital addition to enhance Jessica, a device to guarantee astonishment in those she met.

'Surely you don't have a daughter that age? You look far too young.'

But with Christy comparisons would be made. Even Frank, looking through photographs of a recent holiday, pursed his lips and whistled.

'Well, I don't know where the others came from, but Christy, well, this photograph could be of you in your teens, except that Acid House logo wasn't invented then.'

Christy walked around Mick's garden and the midges swooped lower than swallows in the dusk. Above her the trees creaked and expanded towards the clearing, casting a veil of deciduum through their branches. There were no trees outside the house in Lynton where she had grown up, and at the lake they were still saplings. Unused to the creaking voices of old trees, she shivered, clasping her arms close to her as she looked up to a canopy of leaves. Mick's lawn was as wild as the wood beyond and Christy wove a path back and forth to skirt the brambles leaning in from the wall. A damp scent of nettles hung across the gateway, their green a bright blur in the dying light. Arms bare, hair a blunt gleam on her back, Christy was out of place and small in this wilderness. She was not good at being alone, her steps were hesitant, her body tensed against imagined terrors. At home if Frank was out she spent the evening on the telephone to Maisie or a friend because she didn't really believe she existed if no one was there to see her.

Her dress danced out of the evening when she turned back towards the cottage; in the kitchen steam rolled up to the ceiling from a pan on top of the chipped stove.

Mick was muttering a line of the recipe he was reading, repeating it like a mantra.

'"Blanch and pour, blanch and pour." Here, sweetheart, have a drink for me.' He passed Christy a cloudy glass and went on chanting, "Blanch and pour, blanch and pour."'

The wine stung her throat and she felt it sliding down, weighty and rotund as if she were swallowing an oyster. Suffocation crept over her again and she kicked off her shoes and lay on the sofa. She knew what was really troubling her. It was Friday, she wasn't working on Saturday, although she often did, and neither was Mick. She had no way of getting home unless Mick decided to take her. She was stuck and she was going to sleep with him. That was why she was here. It wasn't that she didn't want to do it, she had come knowing this would happen. She crushed a cushion against herself and longed for it to be over, to have done it so it could never be the first time again.

Mick laid the table with candles while Christy sat like a stone, Hotspur's head resting on her lap. The scar on Mick's forehead turned red as the sun lingered on the front window. It was already dark on the other wall and the last rays waned, shrinking the room towards Mick and Christy facing one another in the glowing window. Mick ate her food as well as his own, holding his fork like a shovel as she had been taught never to do, wiping the plate clean with bread and rubbing his hands across his mouth when he had finished; she half expected him to burp and push his plate back but he leant his elbows on the table and picked his teeth instead. Christy pushed some grains of rice around her plate then smoked four cigarettes in a row. She could never eat with Mick. His vast appetite swallowed hers, and his energetic pursuit of every morsel repelled her, making food something too physical for her to bear.

Mick finished cleaning his teeth and left the table to light the fire. He crouched on the hearth breaking kindling, light as a cat on his feet even though he was filling the whole fireplace with his body. Christy tiptoed past Mick's turned back and tucked herself into the chair by the fire.

'What do you think of this place, sweetheart? Do you like it out here in the sticks?' His voice was smooth as glass to steady her now they had moved from the table.

In the half light he loomed and Christy receded sinking back in monochrome shadows, her pink dress the only colour in the room. She didn't answer.

Mick laughed.

'Are you still here, Christy? I can't see you now, and I can't hear you. You're scared as all hell, aren't you?'

'I'm not scared, I'm nervous.'

'Same thing,' said Mick and he stretched out on the sofa, leaning back to look at her bolt upright on her chair near the fireplace.

She wished he would turn the lights on. The heap of him merged with the heap of sofa, spreading across the whole room. Neither of them spoke. And then Mick was holding her hands and his hands were so warm she realised hers were frozen. And he was putting his arms around her, unbending her clamped elbows and wrapping her arms around him. And he was kissing her, making her feel so wanted that she did not notice that she wasn't nervous any more.

Christy woke up stretching in warm morning light. She was in Mick's bedroom and the telephone was ringing downstairs. She heard him answer it, his voice clear at first then rumbling indistinct but constant like a train passing. She couldn't help smiling, thinking that even at seven-thirty he couldn't stop talking.

He appeared in the bedroom, dressed and wide awake.

'You get up early.' Christy pulled the sheets up to her face, self-conscious at being naked in daylight when Mick had clothes on. He smelt of coffee when he kissed her. 'I thought you'd be asleep. I have to collect something now, so I'll be seeing you later, sweetheart.' He stroked her hair and was gone.

Christy rolled over and closed her eyes, listening to the car roar away until the sound was so distant it mingled with the moving trees.

From the beginning of the trial everyone knew I was Mick's girlfriend. The policemen with macho guns who guarded every entrance, the court clerks, even the traffic warden, who had stopped giving me tickets when a constable told him who I was. They smiled at me with sad sympathy in their eyes and whispered 'Poor love' when I passed.

Mick was delighted.

'It'll really help the atmosphere with the jury and their mood and all that if everyone feels sorry for you, sweetheart,' he told me during one of our visits.

'But I don't know if they're sorry for me because of what might happen to you or because I'm involved with you.'

Mick stretched his fingers under the glass screen and touched my hand.

'It doesn't matter what they're thinking. Just look tragic and wronged as often as you can and be drop-dead sexy the rest of the time. They'll love you, Christy, they'll love you.'

He pressed his palm flat against the glass and I did the same, my hand fitting into his so it looked as though I'd drawn round it. This was how we held hands now.

Mick liked being in court. Right from the first day he had power even though he was handcuffed. The security around his case was crazy. Even the barristers were searched with metal detectors, once at the front door and once outside the courtroom.

Mick applied to the Judge to have the handcuffs removed a week after the case was opened. His arm was sore from the days spent tethered to a shifting rota of police officers.

'It's not as though I'm going to do anything, Your Honour,' he said to the Judge with a grin. I thought he shouldn't be smiling, he should be pleading, but Mick wasn't like that and anyway the Judge almost smiled back. 'I'd have to be crazy, wouldn't I, to think about escaping with two dozen

47

men with guns crawling around this building?' He lifted his right arm, dragging the policeman beside him to reluctant attention. 'I'll be ending up deformed, Your Honour. I'm already blistered and bruised enough – you can see the bandage right here.' He pointed with his unyoked hand at the greying fabric on his captive wrist.

The Judge considered him, head on one side, wig awry, heaped up like suet.

'No, I don't think we'll uncuff you, Mr Fleet.'

Mick scratched his scalp and ran his fingers through his hair slowly; the policeman's hand hovered useless above his own.

'I suppose it might be prejudicial to the prosecution,' said Mick. 'For sure it's prejudicial to the defence that I am handcuffed.'

The Judge straightened up in his chair shaking his head and shuffled small hands among his papers.

'No, Mr Fleet. I cannot allow that. You cannot talk like that in the courtroom.'

I didn't see why it mattered. The jury were always sent out when the Judge and Mick, interrupting his barrister, had this sort of conversation, and they had it often. Mick couldn't help treating the Judge like someone he knew. He was always demanding reasons and explanations for the way things worked. The Judge allowed far more than I expected. He seemed to like Mick, even though Mick was fired up and emotional sometimes.

'This is the rest of my life being debated, Your Honour. I need to know what you all think you're doing with it in here.'

The Judge was like a slap of water in his responses.

'Yes, yes, but you cannot go against the legal structure,' he explained time after time.

Mick had a talent for making other people feel important. He gave me a role when all I really needed was to be there. But maybe he was right to. He sucked me into his trial so deep that I could not have got out if I had wanted to. I didn't want to. I was his route to the outside world, and I was vital. Mr Sindall, Mick's barrister, had a team of solicitors who darted around me nipping information from me before returning to their notes and files. Members of the public who came to watch the trial smiled at me; one or two spoke, just making conversation: 'It's a lovely day,' 'Traffic's bad on the ring road, I hear,' 'Do you know when the canteen opens?' I knew what they were doing. Each sentence came with a searching gaze, their ears flared when I responded and they tucked my words into their gloating minds and hoarded them to tell their friends later. 'I spoke to his girlfriend. She was friendly, not like you'd expect one of them to be.' I could hear them marvelling as if I was with them, back in their safe worlds where court was a source of excitement and glamour. I was a part of that glamour and it would have been a lie to say I didn't love it.

Maisie kept Tuesday evenings free for experimenting on Christy. It was a ritual that had evolved long before Maisie decided that hairdressing was her vocation and before Christy was old enough to understand the repercussions of acquiescence.

Christy was three when Maisie first realised she was better than a doll.

'Christy, of course, can walk and talk and wee very nicely. The only thing she can't do is grow her hair fast,' Maisie explained to their mother in a moment of pride.

Christy basked in a sense of unity with her sister but was anxious. Her hair must grow faster. She tugged at it, she wove nests of wool in its split-ends and filled them with pebbles and buttons as ballast, and she screamed herself breathless blue if Jessica tried to trim it. The hair was a perfect tool for Maisie, a rope to knot, a sheet to drape, a mop to curl. Christy never minded how much Maisie pulled or pinched at her scalp; the habit of pleasing her was unassailable. By the time Christy was seventeen, the habit of pleasing Maisie had lost most of its charm, but she still found herself melting before her sister's jaw-tight determination. She managed to strike a deal for Tuesday nights only and on the whole they had stuck to it.

This Tuesday Maisie was doing hair extensions. Christy found the bottle of wine she had bought rolling like a nine-pin in the back of the fish van and rang Maisie's door bell. Squinting up for the key, Christy stepped back to the edge of the pavement. Her reflection warped in the plate glass of the magic shop on the ground floor of Maisie's building, and again in the distorting mirrors at the back of the shop. Christy bloated, Christy wide-hipped and fish-tailed, Christy long and narrow as a snake, stared back at Christy hot on the pavement.

Danny appeared behind her, his shirt flapping open in the breathless still of the evening. He was back from college for the summer, quiet and etiolated from the months spent bending over his computer. Christy had tried to make him join a circus school she had seen a poster for, but Danny was only interested in computers and making money.

Maisie's key landed in the gutter behind them extravagantly wrapped in a knot of silver satin. She was in a good mood. When she was angry the key hurtled from her third-floor window bound to a lump of coal. She didn't care if she hit anyone, didn't care if she hurt anyone; when Maisie was angry everyone had to know and preferably suffer as well. Much thought accompanied her key in its arc to the pavement; on days of depression there was a damp sponge, on sad days just the key, naked and alone, and on tempestuous days the contents of her handbag showered down, papers and receipts twirling like woodshavings and landing out of reach on the ledge above the magic shop.

'Why does Maisie have to be so affected? I wish she'd lay off.'

Danny tried to throw the slither of ribbon into a dustbin but Christy took it from him.

'She's just like this. You know there's no point in arguing. Anyway, at least she's in a good mood this evening.'

Maisie had laid the kitchen table for supper and pulled the coloured blinds so the room flickered pink and orange like the inside of a Chinese lantern. Her collection of car accessories and bumper stickers crowded the shelves by the cooker and stirring a pan she paused to run a wooden spoon across a row of plastic dogs, setting them nodding manically in time to the tune on the radio.

Christy dropped her scarf on the back of a chair and opened the wine.

'This is really nice, Maisie, what a treat, I didn't expect supper.'

Maisie giggled.

'Look again at the table, Chris.' Her eyes danced and she winked at Danny.

Christy lit the candles and looked. Salad, bread, pots of mustard and relish dotted the table and the plates were prettily decorated with sauces.

'I don't understand.' Christy squinted nearer and squealed. The salad wasn't lettuce, it was green hair, the very hair that Christy was supposed to be wearing later, viscous and apparently doused in dressing. The bread was a hairbrush wrapped in a napkin and the sauces were shampoos and conditioners drifting a sweet synthetic smell across the room. Christy suddenly felt very hungry.

'God, this must have taken you ages.' Walking around the table eyeing the feast, she was annoyed that she could ever have mistaken it for food. Maisie's joke was revolting; Christy couldn't laugh as Maisie and Danny were.

Maisie was almost hysterical, clutching her stomach, knees together, back hunched, so she was a string of knots and curved corners enjoying her own joke with childlike abandon. She hadn't meant it to be creepy. That was the trouble with Maisie: she was always upsetting people without meaning to, especially people close to her. Ben was lucky to live in the middle of the North Sea; on days when Maisie really lost control Christy liked to imagine her sailing off to join him, never coming back, but wreaking red-hot havoc on the oil rigs.

Maisie didn't give Christy hair extensions in the end.

'Your hair is long enough and anyway, I don't think green would really suit you.'

She did it to Danny instead and Christy was her assistant.

He looked like a fairground troll when his sisters had finished soldering seaweed strands on to his dark hair. He posed on the motor bike while Maisie darted round with her comb, flicking wisps of hair into ever more absurd peaks. Christy ached with laughter, wandering through the flat looking for the camera. She was halfway through Maisie's wardrobe, throwing clothes out in a jigsaw swirl of colours, when the door bell rang.

Maisie leaned out of the window dangling the key from a lock of green hair.

'It's Mick.'

'What's he doing here? I didn't even say what I was doing this evening.'

Christy crawled out from the scented folds of Maisie's clothes and ran to look out of the window. The pavement was empty. Mick was already in the building.

Danny scuttled in from the living room, his neck pushed down into his shoulders, trying to hide his head like a tortoise.

'Get this crap off me. I'm not your doll, you know.' Grabbing Maisie's scissors he slammed himself inside the bathroom.

Christy stared in astonishment at both the doors, the front one through which Mick was about to appear and the bathroom one echoing with Danny's anger.

'I don't think he wants cool Mick to see him dressed up as My Little Troll,' whispered Maisie.

Mick was breathless and had running clothes on when he opened the door. Sweat glistened on his forehead and his eyes gazed blank and tired. Christy was disappointed: Mick should be equal to anything. And he shouldn't wear tracksuits. No one should wear tracksuits.

She stepped back from him.

'How did you know I was here?'

Mick ignored her and tried to open the bathroom door. 'Danny's in there, you'll have to wait.'

Christy followed him into the kitchen and gave him a tea towel to wipe his face on. His skin was pasty white and looked as if it would crumble like cheese if he rubbed it. She averted her eyes. He drank a pint glass of water in one slide and revived, wetting his hair under the kitchen tap so he looked like a boxer with the tea towel slung around his neck. It was better than looking like a jogger.

'Your dad told me you were coming round here. I thought I'd drop by and make sure your sister wasn't pulling out your teeth.'

Maisie glared at him and Christy laughed, pleased he had come charging in to find her like a knight in shining armour.

'Why would she be?'

'Well, when your dad said she was doing some kind of experiments on you I wasn't sure what he was meaning, so I thought I'd get myself here and find out.' He grinned at Maisie who raised her chin and scowled disdain.

'I've got a different victim tonight, actually,' she said. 'But he's not very open-minded.'

Danny came out of the bathroom with his hands concealed inside a nest of slithering green and his hair one jagged inch long.

Maisie screamed and stamped her foot.

'You little bastard. That took hours to do. That hair cost a fortune and you've just cut it all off because you didn't think you looked cool enough.' She slapped the wet hanks into the sink and burst into tears. Danny reached out a hand to her to say sorry but she pulled away, saliva a reptilian gleam on her lips. 'Fuck off.

I'll never forgive you, so don't even try to say sorry.'

Another door slammed, this time Maisie's bedroom. Mick whistled.

'Well, she's got a temper in her to stop rivers, hasn't she?'

Danny was by the sink, mute and defenceless as a shadow, looking down at Maisie's hair extensions beached above the waterline on dirty pans and plates. He was almost crying. Christy put her arms round him.

'Come on, Danny, you know she doesn't mean it. Let's go to the pub for a bit. When we come back she'll have forgotten about it.'

Mick didn't want to let it go.

'You shouldn't be having her do that to you, Danny. Tell her to say sorry now, tell her to act up or she'll be in a load of big trouble.'

Christy noticed for the first time in a while how strong Mick's accent was. Maybe he sounded more Irish because someone else was there. On her own with him Christy was not conscious of his voice at all. It was as if they communicated without talking much, but that couldn't be right because Mick had to talk all the time; if he didn't he would explode.

They went to the pub at the bottom of Maisie's road and Mick left them at a table and went to the bar. Danny rolled a cigarette thin as a pipe cleaner and lit it perched on a windowsill. Smoking with his chin tucked into the collar of his shirt and his hair dripping down his neck, he shivered and clenched his teeth. Christy squeezed his hand across the table.

Mick returned with the drinks wedged in a lopsided triangle between his hands, and sat down next to Danny.

'Do you want to come with me to meet some bikers on Thursday? I'm doing a kind of story on them and I heard there was a meeting going on near Wisenton. We could go and see what they're all about.'

Danny shed his gloom and sat up, his spirits lifting as confidence bolstered him and his gestures became emphatic.

'Tell me more about what you do. Chris hasn't said anything and it must be really interesting.'

'I don't know anything, he hasn't told me.' Christy glared at Mick.

He took her hand and kissed it.

'I got into the whole thing because I like taking pictures and I used to go all over to do it. You meet people, you get talking in bars and sometimes something comes of it, you know.'

Christy went to get the next round of drinks, weaving though groups of people to the bar, taking her time so Mick and Danny could talk. It was easier to ask Mick questions with Danny asking too. Alone his intensity bore down on her, crushing her own thoughts until she had nothing to say.

Mick wanted Danny to come back to the cottage with them. Christy felt guilty about Maisie.

'I'll go back and stay with her,' she said when they reached Mick's car, but Mick handed Danny the keys and opened the back door.

'Come on, sweetheart, I need you to hold my hand now while this speed freak takes us home.'

Danny pulled a yellow note from the windscreen.

'You've got a ticket. Bad luck.' He stretched to pass it to Mick then pulled it back frowning. 'Hang on, there aren't any restrictions here after six, so how come they've given you this? Hey, it says four o'clock; you weren't here then,

56

were you?' Danny slid into the driver's seat muttering about traffic wardens.

Mick shoved the ticket in his pocket.

'Calm you down, Danny boy. I parked here earlier and left the car while I went around town a bit, that's all.'

In the back seat Christy lolled her head on Mick's shoulder, warm and happy with his arm around her. She looked up at him.

'Well, how did you see Dad then?' Her voice was lazy as she twisted herself until she was comfortable resting against his side.

Mick's arm tensed and his frame was as unyielding as metal beside her. He sighed, pressing his fingers knuckle white on the back of the driver's seat.

'I never said I saw your dad, girl, I called him up. Is that OK with you? Now stop policing me. Turn right here, Danny. *Right*, I said. Jesus, will we be living after this journey is the question now.' He hugged both arms around Christy, and the car spat dust on to the twilight road.

5

Christy did not enhance her mother's beauty like Maisie and Danny. Their colouring, their tall grace set off Jessica's moon cool to perfection. Christy tagged along behind her mother, anxious to please her. It was like chasing a shadow: no matter how hard Christy tried, she could not make her mother turn to her with the easy affection of childhood.

Christy was fifteen when she began to understand how her mother hated getting old and blamed her for it. There was a shopping trip Christy remembered. It began badly. Danny was away camping with a friend, so everything he needed for school had to be selected by his sisters. Maisie headed with unerring eye for the most expensive version of school trainers, sweatshirts and tracksuits, sneering and mocking her mother as she searched through the sale racks. Christy darted back and forth between them, trying to divert Maisie's lashing scorn, glancing anxiously at her mother whose brow creased deep and then deeper when she saw Christy watching her.

Jessica's mood changed when they left the department store, Danny's uniform parcelled and awaiting collection later. She linked arms with her daughters, and smiled, pulling them forward to giggle at a window where a youth blushed in his struggle to pull tights over the stiff legs of a naked mannequin. Their heads together laughing, embracing in the street, the reflection in the shop window was of three girls. Jessica saw this when she threw back her head and her veins raced with triumph. Her daughters hovered on the brink of womanhood and she was forty and still as slight and graceful as they were.

She hugged them both closer and said, 'I'm going to do it. I want to buy you each a grown-up party dress. It's my own money, left by my aunt, and it's time you each had something special.'

Maisie hardly waited for her to finish speaking.

'God, thanks, Mum. I know what I want. Come in here, quick.' She dragged her mother and sister into a small shop where music throbbed from the open door.

Jessica was disconcerted. She had imagined they would go and drink coffee first, and talk about where they might go, what they might buy. A cloud of femininity and fashion talk would roll over them and the occasion would be marked with celebration. But that was not Maisie's way. She smiled as her elder daughter came out of the changing room pirouetting, a skin of gold hardly covering her. It wasn't possible for Maisie to wait and talk, she was too impulsive.

'What do you think, Mum?' Maisie snaked her spine high and tiptoed in front of the mirror, holding her hair up with both hands, twisting so she could see her back. The colour flowed down from her hair into her dress, shifting like scales in the light.

Jessica blinked.

'You look lovely, darling, but isn't it a bit short?'

Christy nudged her.

'Don't say that, Mum, she'll just try and find a shorter one.'

Maisie stalked back into the changing room, her voice shrill above the music.

'This is the one I want. I don't like anything else. I'm not forcing you to buy me a dress, you offered.'

Christy and Jessica looked at one another. Jessica winked.

'You know her better than I do,' she whispered, and they giggled.

The dress was folded in tissue paper, turned over and over like pastry until a square, white and neat as a pie, lay on the counter. Christy fidgeted, anticipation surging for her turn, her mouth dry when Jessica wrote the cheque for Maisie's dress.

'It doesn't matter, I don't need anything if we can't afford it.'

But Jessica snapped shut her bag and squeezed Christy's arm.

'Nonsense, darling, of course you are having a dress too. Now come on, where shall we go?'

Maisie skipped ahead, shouting ideas back at Jessica and Christy strolling, talking in low voices behind her. In the next shop Jessica searched through the rails for garments she imagined were appropriate for a fifteen year old. Christy was thrilled at her mother's interest and took armfuls into the changing room, emerging sporadically, hunched and embarrassed, in a succession of sequins and frills.

'Mum doesn't know what I want,' she whispered to Maisie.

'Try this.' Maisie passed her a handful of gauze.

In the cubicle Christy slipped the dress over her head and came out to show her mother and Maisie before she looked at it herself. Jessica turned towards her and gasped. Christy saw her mother's face crumble, eyes staring from pinched tight skin, sallow and old as if a wax had spilt across her features. She moved in front of the mirror, trying to keep her shoulders straight and her head up.

'Don't you like it, Mum?'

Tears dazzled Jessica's vision. Christy's soft shoulders rose clear in her mind, and Christy's face framed by white blonde hair, the dress in shades of grey like the dawn. She saw a reflection of herself except that the self she saw had not existed for twenty years. Her earlier triumph of sisterhood with her daughters was confounded now; she moved and stood beside Christy, forcing herself to mark the contrast further. Christy's skin was mapped with veins so fine it looked as though she had been burnished to the point of transparency. Beside her Jessica sagged from her spine, shrouded by years of dust and dullness, heavy, sucking light in instead of giving it out. She was old and she resented Christy for reminding her of it.

Christy watched her mother's face in silence. She had done something dreadful. The dress was wrong.

'I don't really like this one,' she whispered.

'Rubbish, you look great.' Maisie swung her round. 'This is the one. Come on, Mum, let's buy it and go and have some lunch.'

The shop assistant bustled over.

'You must be proud of her,' she said as she chivvied Christy into the changing room. 'You must have looked just like her in your heyday.'

Jessica nodded and tried to smile.

Christy never wore the dress while her mother was alive.

*   *   *

61

Through the summer Christy worked long hours on the fish farm and Mick was often away. She borrowed Frank's van and drove to the cottage at dusk when the last angler had left the lake, his rods and nets bundled in the boot of his car, his fish slithering and drying on the seat beside him. When Mick was away, Christy went to his cottage to look after his dog. Hotspur stayed with her the first time Mick went away, but he pined, scratching and whining, never able to be still. Frank did not like dogs and had replaced Jessica's pair of black pugs with a sigh of relief and a pale hall carpet when they followed her to the grave. He grunted and didn't look up from his paper when Christy told him that Mick's dog was coming to stay. But once Hotspur was installed his reed-thin voice rose through the house like dust reaching every corner when he was parted from Christy, and Frank stopped grunting and shouted instead.

'Get that damned thing out of here. I caught it eating the bonemeal around the roses this morning. It dug one up. You are not keeping it under control, Christy. I won't put up with it any longer.' Frank glared at Hotspur as he spoke; Hotspur licked his lips and curved himself in apology, scraping across the lawn towards the crinoline shade of a rose bush.

Christy caught him and shut him in the garden shed, but he climbed up to the window and stood craning his neck, following Christy everywhere with his pleading eyes. It was better to keep him at Mick's cottage.

Mick was never gone for more than three or four days, and when Christy was busy at the lake, Danny was there, on holiday from college, and he liked to take the van and speed off to feed the dog, freedom a plume of exhaust smoke behind him.

Frank was making money now from the fish farm. His overdraft no longer ballooned each month and he forgot that he was lonely and bereaved when he looked out at

62

the land through which his business flowed as strong as the narrow stream that fed his lakes. The wounds which had ridged the earth around the lakes were healed now and small trees shivered a path up to the office. Frank's island with its top-knot of reeds and grasses tangling with bramble hoops rustled with purpose as beasts and birds threaded their way through the scrub. From the porch Frank trailed them with his binoculars before dusk. His ritual coincided with the heron's slow circuit of the lake, and Frank watched the bird land on the shore, long legs crumpling in slow motion, wings beating up air for balance, before it could stand, still and upright as a sentry, except for the bone beak thrusting from the rushes. The heron was a menace on the lakes, dilettante in his clean dive to pierce a fish he didn't want to eat. Flapping back to the shore, his trophy impaled and struggling on his beak, he paused and the slick black marking on his head was an eyebrow raised in challenge to Frank, impotent by the house.

Christy felt that at last after almost three years the house was beginning to become a place where people were happy. At first it had been too new and too soon; the rooms were sharp with pain and there were not enough cushions or pictures and no happy memories to soften them. Frank had begged Maisie to come home, even for a short time, but she had said no. She hadn't understood how much they needed her to be there for a while so that this house could fill with images and sounds and life. Christy knew that deep down her father missed Maisie and her jangling energy, as he missed Jessica. With Danny away half the year Christy couldn't fill the spaces left around her father. And meeting Mick made it worse. Christy hated leaving Frank when she went out with Mick. Most of all she hated it when Frank waved them off and she could still see him smaller and smaller, sitting with the newspaper alone on the porch.

It was Christy's idea to build the porch. It was a proper American one, the kind they had in westerns where mothers sat in rocking chairs and sewed and fathers kicked off their boots after a hot day on the ranch.

Frank didn't want it at first.

'It's going to cost a lot of money just to give you a place to sit three times a year when it's warm enough,' he complained to Christy, but she wouldn't give up.

'It's for you, not me. You can sit and look over the lakes. You must do it, Dad. You can't live here properly unless you have a place you can look out from.'

In the end Frank capitulated, and although he pretended he still thought it a waste of money, Christy found him with the plans, adding steps and widening posts until it stopped being Christy's porch and became part of Frank's house.

Red and low like a barn, the house stood on a bulge in the ground above the main lake. The porch broke up the long side wall and its weather-bleached timber made everything new and just finished look old and permanent. In the roof, bedrooms with pointed ceilings faced out above the porch, window frames curved like plough yokes over glass which time would twist and warp. The house was Frank's surrogate wife and he treated it with the clichéd romance that he had long ago stopped offering Jessica. Every week, he came home from Lynton with flowers. Sometimes he gave them to Christy saying, 'These are to go on the kitchen windowsill and those are for the sitting room,' so she knew they were not meant for her.

Once, after a trip abroad, Frank unwrapped ornaments like jewels: a red glass inkwell, oily as a boiled sweet, a pair of emerald flutes to hold single roses, a tear-shaped turquoise ashtray. He arranged them on a small table, placing them then standing back, pushing them an invisible distance then standing back again, in a trance until they sparkled in an arc around the photographs of Jessica on their wedding day. Christy watched him from the hall. He didn't know she was there and she couldn't disturb him even though a man was waiting to see him. Later, when Frank had gone out to the lake, she pulled a chair up to the little table and sat down in front of her laughing mother. Sunlight tilted through the glass ornaments leaving a rainbow smudge on the table. A tiny insect landed, its body a pea-green glow between transparent wings, whirling as it changed its mind and flew off again. Christy leant back in her chair and closed one eye and for a moment before the sun was swallowed up by cloud she could see Jessica dancing in red and turquoise.

That summer there was no rain for six weeks. The lakes sank as the sun scorched rays across the baked earth and the trout hid themselves in cool deep hollows. Christy helped a small boy dig for worms while his father was fishing, but there were none; they too had forced their way deeper down, to a subterranean layer where soil was damp. The first fishermen arrived at dawn, and Christy woke every morning to the purr of an engine, the clunk of a car door closing.

She asked Frank to restrict the hours.

'I had to get up at five today, Dad. Can't we stop them coming so early?'

But Frank laughed.

'It's good for you, and we'll lose business if we don't let them come early. It's too hot to fish during the day. The trout won't rise.'

He was right. Walking out as the sun rose, rubbing her

eyes, Christy was glad she had to be up. White mist lay over the water and low across the fields, rising to drape tree trunks, thinning in patches warmed by the sun. Her feet left a dark trail through dew-powdered grass as she walked around the lake to a solitary fisherman. A clatter of beating wings broke the silence and three ducks skidded on to the water shouting a warning to one another as they landed. She recognised the fisherman as a regular, and passed him with a professional blinkered smile and muttered greeting. Frank insisted that all members were greeted, and if no one was in the office when they arrived, Christy had to walk around both lakes making sure they had seen her.

'It means they know we know they are fishing; there are always some who want to poach, and this stops them.'

This technique seemed to work. The last time Christy had had to stop a fisherman and ask to look in his bag was three months ago. She remembered it with a shudder. Usually when she thought someone was poaching she called Frank to deal with them, but on this occasion he was away. The man had not been to the lake before; he arrived early, paid a day's membership fee and settled himself on the far side of the big lake. Christy hadn't taken much notice of him. Her paperwork preoccupied her, and the book-keeper had come. But at five o'clock he appeared outside the office to pay for his catch. Christy smiled and went out to greet him. His pale round eyes gazed from a face sprouting hairs, some on the chin, more on his upper lip and a fringe on each cheekbone like low-slung false eyelashes.

'I've just had the two,' he said, pulling a pair of rainbow trout from his fishing bag.

As he held them out to her the bag slipped from his shoulder and landed open at her feet. Inside, fishtails and eyes and pink open mouths heaved, bodies flapped, dry-scaled and dull with exhaustion. He had not even killed them.

'What about those then?' Christy's voice spat anger. She would have let him go; she hadn't noticed the bulge of his fishing bag tucked behind him. Her rage was at her own inefficiency more than his deception. She grabbed the bag and counted. 'One, two, three, four, five . . . you know we only allow three. The rest should have been thrown back.' She spoke to a space.

The man had gone, his plump hips wiggling as he trotted away to his car, throwing the two trout he had declared over his shoulder as he went. Christy gazed after him, her arms full of thrashing fish, astonished by his cowardice.

'You should at least have the guts to stand up for yourself,' she yelled as the car plunged up the track and away.

Christy was confused by Frank's quick fondness for Mick. It made her feel as if they were married already. Already. How could she think 'already' when it was August and she had only known him since May? Mick was often early to collect her. Frank would let him in and lead him through to the porch for a drink. The third time Mick was early Frank didn't even bother to call Christy. Usually he shouted up the stairs, 'Christy, your young man is here.' Mortifying; in the mirror Christy's face flared crimson hot, imagining what Mick must be thinking. The day Frank didn't call up to her she was even more irritated. Did he think Mick had come to see him? Had Mick come to see him? She might as well stay upstairs. No one would notice. She hadn't dressed after her bath yet, but was lounging on her bed, the warm air drying her skin. In the blue light of her room with curtains drawn, her draped limbs gleamed and her stomach and hips curved across the bedspread, taut like the underbelly of a salmon.

She looked down at her body, half closing her eyes, trying to make herself sink and vanish into the deep-water folds of fabric on the bed.

Finally she dressed and went downstairs, moving quietly through the house to surprise Mick and Frank. She saw them and her urge to disturb them slid away. They were so comfortable talking, leaning side by side on the rails of the porch, looking out through the heat-hazed evening. She and Mick didn't go out that night. Frank poured her a drink and took one of her cigarettes even though he never smoked; Christy perched on a basket chair, smooth and grown-up in her father's house. Everything was a little different that evening, like a familiar face subtly altered after a long absence. The shadows and the smells suggested a mood she hadn't known in this house. Cosy domesticity had been Jessica's creation, and it had died with her. When they were alone together, Christy cooked her father instant food in the microwave and they ate it on their knees in front of the television or standing up in the kitchen between forays out to the lake to deal with late fishermen. Frank didn't seem aware of any change, though, leaning back in his chair on the porch, one hand shading his eyes, the other tipping whisky around his glass. Maybe the difference was that she was seeing it all through Mick's eyes. She felt suddenly as if she was looking down at herself, except it wasn't Christy, it was Jessica, and her clothes hung in the way that they used to hang on Jessica, sliding over her frame, never crumpled, never tight.

Frank coughed.

'Are you sure you won't have a drink, Mick? You won't be driving, after all.'

Mick shook his head, staring at Christy, and she came back to life with a shock. She thought she had heard Frank ask Mick to stay the night, but it must have been a mistake. Mick winked at her, his face lit triumphant at Frank's words, but he shook his head.

'I've got the dog to be thinking of, I can't leave him. I'll keep off the alcohol, thanks.'

Christy wondered if Frank had forgotten Mick didn't drink.

They had supper cooked by Frank and it was trout from the lake. Christy gutted it fast and clean, proud of her skill. Mick almost gagged when she drew a line along the belly with her knife and it sprang red teeth like a zip. The flesh parted easily and the fish lay open: a pink feather, the spine a gleam dotted crimson until Christy washed the blood away.

'Don't you like fish, Mick?' she teased. 'You'll have to get used to it if you don't want to starve around here.'

Frank didn't usually talk much in the evenings. Christy worried that he never went anywhere and saw no one except her and the fishermen from week to week, but when she asked him if he was lonely he smiled.

'Not everyone needs to go out to a pub, you know. I like to be here at home, and if you're here too I like it even better. Sometimes.' He paused, Christy went on anxiously twiddling her hair. 'But I can live without seeing you. In fact it wouldn't suit me at all to have you or Danny and Maisie hanging over me every night. I'm used to my own company now.'

But this evening Frank was different. He had his sleeves rolled up to the elbow for rinsing the fish and he didn't fasten them again but kept his arms bare. His arms were wide and freckled under soft hairs. He seemed young and untroubled, the same age as Mick, not another generation. Christy laid the table on the porch and the anti-mosquito light came on, its whip-crack as much a part of summer now as the throb of crickets or the sharp scent of lemon juice which Maisie gave her for her hair. She heard Mick and Frank coming through the house, trays clinking behind their voices.

'Saunders. '77.'

'Arsenal. Crane, Blackburn.'

''78. Mac Rae, Rangers.'

''82 and '83. He scored that goal against Man United in the quarter finals. D'you remember?'

The football litany, that was what Jessica used to call it. Ever since Danny went to his first football match aged six, Christy had heard this conversation. Even when she was small and she knew her father was infallible, she had found it moronic. Jessica loathed it, and banned them from speaking at the table if they so much as mentioned football. But often after supper, when Maisie and Christy were doing their homework and Jessica lay on the sofa trying to read, beneath her fat pugs, they would start again, whispering at first but forgetting when Danny got to his favourites, shouting, 'Wright. Chelsea. '89.' You couldn't even win the game, it was just a list which could be added to until you got bored. Christy was contemptuous.

Mick laughed at her clenched face.

'Sorry, sweetheart. We were just keeping ourselves going in the kitchen. We won't inflict you with it any more.'

Frank put down the knives and forks.

'He's good, you know, Chris, and he can beat me hands down at the rugby version.'

Mick drank water, Frank and Christy consumed two bottles of wine and were buoyant, setting Mick thumping the table with laughter as they described Maisie's initial reaction to the fish farm and her subsequent conversion to its favour.

'She loves it now, of course.' Frank poured more wine. 'Because she knows that if my income is better she can twist my arm and my heartstrings until hers is better too.' He laughed and wiped his face with his handkerchief, changing the subject completely. 'So come on, Mick, tell me how you got that scar, and don't fob me off.'

Mick said nothing. He sipped his water, swallowing audibly, and still said nothing.

Christy gabbled, desperate for there to be no silence.

'I think it's got something to do with you not drinking. I bet you had a fight when you were young and used to get drunk.' She leaned towards him, putting her hand on his arm to pull him closer, wanting to kiss him, even though her father was opposite.

But she was pushed away, steered upright in her place again.

'Lay off, Christy, you don't know what you're talking about.' Mick turned to Frank, making his shoulder a barrier Christy couldn't pass. 'I don't talk about it, Frank, but I know I can tell you and it will go no further.'

Christy heard him like the hurtling of an unstoppable lorry and shut her eyes, hoping to avoid catastrophe. Mick had misread Frank. Frank didn't like lawless stories; you couldn't tell them to him. Mick was going to say something awful and Frank would ban him from the house and from seeing her. Her eyes were creased tight shut so green shapes swam in her head and her ears rang.

Through the ringing came Mick's voice soft and so beguiling you would die for him.

'I was in Romania and I was involved in some of the action for a bit. A lot of people were killed, and I was lucky to get away so lightly. That's all.'

71

Frank was enthralled, demanding more information, more details. Mick sounded like a soldier now, with his talk of rebels and raids and strikes. Christy opened her eyes and the black-blue sky spun with stars. She shut them again. Rage turned the green shapes into black shoals behind her eyelids. How could Mick lie like this to her father? How could she stop him? Slowly, staggering and bumping, she felt her way to the porch railings. Beyond them the ground folded down to the lake, soft black meeting the water without a seam in the dark.

Frank and Mick weren't interested in her; they were two little boys playing fantasy war games. She hated Mick for duping her father, she hated her father for falling for Mick's wiles. She heard their voices sinking lower into the table as they talked. Leaning on the railings she tried to breathe in the summer night and calm down. Nothing happened. Christy thought it must be the drink playing games and she tried again, but her breath went straight out as if she had a puncture. Panic crept up on her. She didn't know what was happening. Why couldn't she breathe? Dizzy and gasping she crashed on to a chair, her hands pushing at her throat, trying to make a space for air to squeeze through.

Mick was beside her almost before she'd sat down.

'Calm down, baby, calm down, you'll be OK. You need to concentrate all your thoughts on breathing. Come on, try and breathe in slowly, slowly.'

Left alone at the table with smeared plates and his glass, Frank became bored.

'Stop that romantic stuff, you two, it's not polite to your poor father. Christy, come and sit here with me again.'

Christy could hear Mick and see him, but she couldn't do what he told her to. When she tried to breathe the puncture was still there and the more she tried the more she couldn't. Her eyes warped with tears from heaving non-breaths.

'What's going on?' Frank peered over Mick's shoulder.

'She's hyperventilating. It's OK. She needs a glass of water and a paper bag.'

Frank pulled himself together, shaking off the wine slur and reminiscences, and sprang into the house muttering, 'Paper bag, paper bag, what's she going to do with a paper bag?' The item was found in the larder; he emptied the bag and brought it back to Mick. 'Is this right?'

Mick nodded and held it up to Christy's mouth. It smelt of onions and was soft and crumpled.

'Blow into this, Christy. Blow into this and see if you can inflate it for me.'

Eyes bulging, cheeks like snooker balls, Christy blew and blew. Frank crouched behind Mick, hands on his knees, glasses on his forehead, observing. Christy knew she couldn't be dying because she wanted to laugh: Frank looked so solemn and so absurd, like a wicketkeeper preparing to field. She inflated the bag and her breathing became deeper and slow. It was over.

'Well done.' Mick held her hand. 'She needs some sleep now.'

Frank kissed her forehead.

'Good-night, Chris, mind you don't do that again, we've run out of paper bags.'

Christy nearly smiled and followed Mick up to her room.

'Get into bed now, sweetheart. You'll be fine now again. I'll see you tomorrow.'

She shivered, Mick wrapped her bedspread around her and kissed her. Mummified in pink candlewick, she struggled to sit upright.

'You didn't get your scar from being a soldier, did you?

I wonder if you'll ever tell me what really happened.' She was warm now and too tired to be angry. Her eyelids sloped down and she flopped against Mick.

Hugging her, he whispered, 'I wonder if I will. Maybe I have, but for sure it doesn't matter a lot, does it? I'm going home now, sweetheart. Good-night.'

He got up then and left. The room, which had been cramped with Mick there, was empty and cold without him.

Mick was public property in court. Everyone had come to see him win or lose, they didn't mind which, they were there for the spectacle. The jury sat in two rows opposite the public gallery and their eyes and heads switched from Mick to the Judge like spectators at a tennis match. I tried to imagine the lives each one of them led. The man in tweeds at the front was the foreman. His pointed nose jutted beneath a green plastic visor which he sometimes pushed up on to his forehead so it became a septic halo around his baldness. He never smiled at Mick, only at the Judge; he never looked at me. The two women on his left could have been sisters, but I don't suppose they were. Both permed, both sucking mints behind pearlised pursed lips and nudging one another when I came into court. Ther eyes snapped malice at first, but Mick worked on them, glancing up to look straight at them when he said something that anywhere else would have been funny. They thawed, and through the endless stifled days they began to like Mick. I could tell by the way their jaws softened and their arms and perhaps their prejudices unbent until it was the Judge they glared at, not Mick. Behind them a young man, black-haired and sallow, smirked and flirted with the girl next to him. She wore pink-rimmed glasses and her nose was stippled like lemon rind. They thought they were really cool and I thought they were sleeping together. The young man didn't like Mick, he didn't like the way Mick could hold his audience when he talked, he didn't like Mick's accent or his scar. I could tell because although he listened without fidgeting to the prosecution, and even to Mick's barrister, when Mick said something he began to fiddle with his pen or loosen his tie. The girl wanted to like Mick, she simpered when he made jokes, but the creep's mouth was never far from her ear, whispering something to make her lip curl in a sneer

75

as she unconsciously moved on her chair so she was nearer him; further from Mick.

Every day for four weeks I sat opposite these people whose names I did not know, watching them decide Mick's future. I stared so hard I sometimes wept, tears from the strain of not blinking stinging my eyes red. Another young man looked like a student: he had acne and greasy hair and I felt sorry for him. He needed to be out in the May sunshine healing his skin and laughing. He frowned through the trial, but not at anyone in particular. I couldn't tell what he was thinking. The man I liked best had silver hair down to his collar and a nose like a Roman. I thought he was an art-school lecturer or a philosopher or something exotic and sympathetic. He sat with his arms folded and his glasses well down his nose and he seemed to be saying, 'Enough of this nonsense, let's talk about life.'

When Mr Sindall described Mick's work, how he learnt to take photographs by lurking on popular beaches with a camera, snapping tourists and then selling them the pictures, the silver-haired man smiled and rubbed his eyes as if he was straightening out a memory. All the time Sindall was building up an image of Mick's struggle to break into reporting, the man was leaning forward on his elbows, dangling his glasses from his finger and thumb, searching Mick's frozen face. I wondered if he could see him at all without his glasses on.

Tobin, the prosecuting counsel, fat and blotched by frustration and too much good living, bounced up and down with objections.

'The defendant's attempts to get work in his teens can hardly be of relevance, Your Honour.'

But the Judge swept him away.

76

'Mr Fleet is presenting his life. We need to know him, Mr Tobin, before we can judge him.'

The silver-haired man liked that and so did I.

Sometimes it was so boring in court that I wanted to stand up and scream. One old lady in the jury nodded off every afternoon about half an hour after we all returned from the lunchtime break, another doodled in her notebook, her fingers twitching to be at her knitting or digging her garden. An old man with the unravelled face of a drinker let his mouth drop open and saliva spill out on a thread. Tobin read out lists of road numbers and map references, car number-plates and witness accounts which hardly varied from, 'The car I saw was dark in colour, I could not say if it was black or not. I could not see the driver. I don't know if there was anyone else in the car. I never saw that car again.'

After court every day I was allowed to go downstairs and see Mick. We talked through the glass screen in the visit cell with two policemen sentinel behind each of us. Mick never cried, neither did I. There wasn't time. We only had half an hour a day, sometimes less when his counsel marched in on a gust of expensive aftershave and politely held the door for me.

'Sorry, Christy, something has come up. Can you see Mick tomorrow?'

Then I waited outside the court for Mick's van to leave to take him back to the prison. I never waited alone. People walking by paused, seeing the police ranked with guns by the gates. They clustered, the way onlookers always do, in a huddle on the corner of the court car-park. I wondered if they had any idea what they were waiting to see. When the gates opened and two motor bikes roared out, followed by a car and then the black-windowed van with Mick somewhere inside it, I felt like a wife at the pit head watching the procession of tragedy. The crowd had the set faces and staring eyes you see in photographs of those disasters as people struggle to comprehend something they cannot imagine.

6

Christy began to think of herself and Mick as one person. What had happened to either of them before was distant and unimportant. When she remembered her life before Mick, she saw drifting images silent and shrunken by the lens of her memory. She was happy now, and it was as if she had never been before. She knew Mick's mannerisms so well that sometimes she thought she had made him up and he could only do what she had imagined him doing. She knew how he whistled to himself almost under his breath when he was concentrating, how he leaned back when he had finished a piece of work and stretched so his spine arched and his hands brushed the swell of the walls. She wished she didn't know how he scratched, and how he bit the skin round his fingernails, so badly they bled and he had to wear plasters. Mick's raw fingertips were ugly. Gloves might help, but she couldn't bring herself to offer them. She didn't like gloves.

One of her earliest memories was of Aunt Vaughan when Danny was a baby, smiling in lipstick as she forced the child's tiny hands into fists, wedging them inside mittens and binding them tight with white ribbon until they waved like clubs above his blanket.

'It stops him clawing his face,' Aunt Vaughan explained as three-year-old Christy stared aghast. 'Babies will claw, you know.' Her lips were a brick slash in her powdered face.

Christy gazed at her brother's flawless cheeks, his feathering lashes. He was asleep, his head and arms thrown back, his mouth open in a small silent gasp. He was round and soft, incapable of such violence. Aunt Vaughan was the one with claws, long pointed nails dipped in blood which she tapped on the table when Danny woke and cried.

'Babies need to cry, it develops their lungs.'

Aunt Vaughan had been there too much when Danny was a new baby. Jessica had needed her best friend to rally her through a difficult birth. Aunt Vaughan had been an actress. She wasn't really their aunt, but Jessica loved her 'like a sister but better'. When they were small, Christy and Maisie were troubled by this phrase. How could you love someone better than a sister? They were sisters. What did Mummy mean? It was never explained. Vaughan was still attached to her stage voice and her vowels swooped and quivered when she drank gin. She drank gin a lot, on her own in the kitchen. Maisie and Christy were too young for school still; Vaughan chivvied them around the house in the mornings and put them to bed in the afternoons. They were afraid of her painted face which smudged and slurred over the cooker as she prepared inedible meals; they were afraid of her tight stiff clothes and her spiked heels which pierced the floor leaving a trail of bullet holes in her wake. Frank stayed later and later at work, Jessica never got out of bed except to snatch Danny from his crib when he cried and wedge a bottle into his screaming mouth. The girls were left with Vaughan. She sliced raw onion into sandwiches for them and dusted her cigarette ash across their beds when she made them in the morning. They longed to see Jessica, but for three weeks after the baby came they were kept from her room.

'Your mother is tired,' Vaughan explained, one long red-laced finger under each of their chins. 'She will see you soon, but not yet.'

Small wonder that they clung to Frank when he left for work each morning and longed for his return in the evening. He read their bed-time stories and mended their dolls. He was kind and dependable. He was their favourite. When Jessica recovered, she came down in her dressing gown and drank with Vaughan in the kitchen. Frank and his small daughters crept round the wall of secret talking which the two women built up, day after day, night after night, glass after glass.

Finally Vaughan left. Jessica thawed and regained colour in her face and her voice. She still spent hours in bed, her hair drifting across her shoulders, her legs a perfect fishtail beneath the grey silk bedspread. Christy would burrow beneath the covers, her small hand seeking the reassurance of her mother's skin; Maisie had told her, 'Mummy turns into a mermaid when she goes to bed,' and Christy needed daily proof that this was not true. They hoped Vaughan would never be back. But once or twice a year Jessica sank again to be rallied each time by a visit or a phone call from Vaughan. The girls were no longer afraid of her. The fear had turned to pity.

One winter afternoon when Christy was ten, Jessica dropped the three children at the garden gate and drove away down the street to deposit the neighbours' children. They filed into the house, banging bags down in the hall. Maisie, aloof now she was at secondary school, ran upstairs to change her clothes, but Christy and Danny barged into the living room to turn on the television. There, unconscious on the floor, they found Vaughan, her skirt rucked, her limbs folded uncomfortably. She had fallen off the sofa, so bolstered by alcohol she had not woken. Like a dead bird she sprawled on the carpet, her mouth half open, her skin tight yellow when they turned on the light.

'She's drunk,' said Danny, prodding her with his toe, 'and it smells in here.'

Christy opened the window to rid the room of the metallic breath emitted by Vaughan's every pore. Vaughan groaned and sat up, blinking, her face sagging and confused, in it a premature glimpse of an old woman. Christy helped her up.

'Dear me, I can't think what happened. Nothing to worry about, children, I was just dozing. Now, I think a sharpener will set me up for the evening.' She swayed out of the room.

Christy watched her go, brittle with cracked dignity, and suddenly she knew she was fond of her.

Since Jessica's death Vaughan had stayed away.

'It's too sad, I can't come back to find Jessica eclipsed,' she sighed on the telephone when Christy rang to thank her for a present.

Christy tried to point out that this was a new house, a new life now, but Vaughan paid no heed.

'Dear Jessica, how I miss her. Do keep in touch, Christy; come and stay with me soon. Remember, as your godmother, it is my duty to protect you.'

Christy didn't think Vaughan would be much use in an emergency. She always wore high-heels and satin-boned dresses as closely related to underwear as dresses could be, but she meant well.

When she was at work and the day crawled, Christy stared out of the office window at the fishermen squatting like stones beside the lake and thought about Mick. At lunchtime he would be writing. He didn't have lunch, he said it slowed him down. He wrote at the table in the main room of his cottage, clearing a small space in the chaos of books and maps and yesterday's newspaper. She could see what he saw when he looked up from his work and turned to gaze out of the window. She could hear his breathing and his footsteps when he got up and went to the door or to answer the telephone; she tried not to ring him up during the day; he sounded further away if she talked to him. If she imagined him instead, the conversation would go her way.

He told her more about his work now, in sentences like banners, floating above their time together. There were two newspapers in Ireland he worked for. Christy wanted to see his pieces on the printed page. He showed her one, a stain of yellow paper with a faded photograph of children tightrope-walking along an army blockade in Belfast. The story was brief reportage and the writer was not named, but along the edge of the photograph in small capitals Christy read Mick's name and pride caught in her throat.

'Show me more, please, Mick,' she begged, expecting a fat book of cuttings to appear.

'I don't keep them,' he said, stretching by the window, reaching his arm back to scratch his shoulder blade then heaving his shoulders up and down as if he were preparing for some weight-lifting.

Christy's time was split now between work and Mick. If she stayed with Mick on weekdays, she rose while he was still sleeping and drove home along roads gleaming ink blue where the sun met the damp skin of tar. On those early morning drives where she saw no one, Christy played back her evening and her night with Mick, and when she reached home it was a wrench like leaving him again to become Christy the fish-farm manager.

Frank was happy for her, but there were evenings when dusk hung on the lake and he was alone, and missing his wife enough to scream, even now, three years on. He didn't want Christy or anyone to know that he couldn't sleep, that he thought about Jessica every five minutes throughout the night. An air of unease stayed with him, only sublimated by work to the point of exhaustion. He could never know Jessica's heart now no matter how he searched his own. He could never know if she would have stayed with him. He smiled when he read in one of Christy's magazines that a man was supposed to think about sex every five minutes. Not love.

Christy lost touch with her friends. She didn't need them. One or two people telephoned, wanting to meet her before they went back to college, but she was busy. Mick's work took him away at short notice; she didn't like to commit herself in advance in case she missed the day he came home.

Maisie teased her.

'If you spend any more time with him you'll start to look like him. You already sound like him.'

'Don't be silly, how can I? He's Irish.' Christy laughed but secretly she was pleased.

Maisie had been away with Ben. He was back from the rigs for two months and Maisie made him take her on holiday.

'If I don't he'll just stay in the flat with that motor bike and rot in its engine until he has to go back.'

They returned home as the summer spilled into September, and Maisie came to the farm straight from the plane to show off her suntan. Christy was on the roof of the office with Danny, nailing down lead flashing, sealing it for winter. Maisie sauntered out to watch them, swinging her hair down her bare back, goosebumps rising on her arms because she was wearing a sundress and the air was cool. Christy's muscles ached from heaving ribbons of lead and her fingers throbbed where the hammer had missed its target too often. Maisie looked pampered and cherished, Ben's car keys hooked like a ring on her finger.

'Come down, leave that stuff. I want to tell you about Spain. Ben gave me a necklace and I've brought it to show you. He's coming in a minute, I dropped him off with Dad by the lake.'

Danny's hammer beat on the roof, its rhythm unchanging as if Maisie wasn't there. He hadn't spoken to her for weeks now: he was still waiting for her to apologise for the hair extensions. Christy wiped her hands on dirty jeans and climbed down. She moved to hug Maisie, leaning into the coconut scent festooning her sister.

Maisie stepped back.

'Oh don't. You're not in the mood, I can see.' She spoke sharply, and her hands flew out to push Christy away.

Christy straightened, flushing, aware of every trickle of sweat, every tickle of dust coating her unclean skin.

'You're right, I am filthy. I'll have a bath when I get in.'

Walking back to the house she stumbled and plodded, earth-bound and troglodyte, next to radiant Maisie.

Ben and Frank edged round each other in the hall. Christy opened the front door and walked straight into Ben. His narrow hands steadied her.

'Hi there, Christy. You look hot.'

Christy kissed him; his cheek was smooth and smelt of cheap aftershave, he was as groomed as Maisie, leaning in immaculate repose against the wall, the toe of one polished cowboy boot extended in front of the other.

Frank didn't like Ben. He didn't want his daughter to marry a welder on an oil rig. Ben said he would give up the oil rigs when they got married. He and Maisie would take the motor bike over to France and ride it round the world. Frank thought this was even worse.

'Where is the security in that? All she would have is a motor-bike helmet. No house, no furniture, nothing.'

Christy tried to soothe him, but seeing Ben and Maisie together always set him off again. 'He is feckless and irresponsible. What does she see in him?' he appealed to Christy after they had left.

Christy turned away to hide her smile. Frank liked Mick. She had got something right where Maisie had got it wrong, and she felt a swoop of triumph. Ben would never give Maisie safety. Christy couldn't imagine wanting anything else.

'No, Dad, that's mean, you can't think like that. They've been together a long time, he really cares about her, it's just that he isn't here much. He isn't ready for a base yet.'

'Well, he isn't ready for marriage then. I just don't think Maisie will be happy.'

He broke off, as Danny came in, a film of sawdust and grime coating his clothes and his hair.

'Danny doesn't think much of him either.'

'Of who?' Danny perched on the edge of the sofa, his feet parked far apart and his elbows on his knees as he leaned to switch on the television with one hand and pour beer into a glass on the floor with the other.

'Maisie's beau.'

'He's better than Maisie,' was all Christy heard before the cricket commentator joined them in the room, his voice amplified and crisp against the soft thwack of the cricket ball and the rattle of applause.

Maisie was dying to come to court and see the action, but she couldn't because the police thought they might use her as a witness. She was thrilled.

'I can't wait to give evidence, it's like being in a film. I hope they don't ask me to say anything awful about Mick, though. Mind you, I never liked him.'

'Maise, please don't start.' I was so tired of hearing her, clear and pure as a church bell in recollecting her prescience. She told Dad that she'd always thought there was something fishy about Mick.

That made me laugh.

'Come on, Maisie, we're all a lot more fishy than Mick, literally.'

One Friday the police decided they didn't want her to give evidence for the prosecution. The next day I went to see Mick in the prison where they were keeping him in the high-security unit. If the defence wasn't going to call Maisie either she could come to court with me on Monday. Mick would know if she was needed. I visited him every weekend during the trial, like I had ever since his arrest. It all took so long. He was on remand for six months before his case was brought to court. They wouldn't give him bail. They said he was too dangerous. He didn't look dangerous to me. I could not reconcile the side I knew of Mick with the evidence shoaling up against him. I pushed away the thought of all that potential guilt when I visited him, I had to.

Going to the prison was my ritual now, like going to Mum's grave. Instead of going to Mum's grave. Driving there I could spot the other girlfriends and wives getting off buses and out of cars and taxis to converge in a fluff of fake-fur coats and powder at the blue steel door. When I first started visiting Mick I was amazed by the other women. They had earrings and lipstick and low-necked dresses. Most of them didn't wear tights and their bare legs puckered purple above scuffed stilettos. The few in dirty jeans and old sweatshirts were signalling the end of their interest in their captive husbands. I never saw them more than once or twice again. The dolled-up ones were constant.

Mick loved me to dress up to visit him.

'You're the only colour in here, Christy, and the only smell that makes me happy.'

I used up a lot of scent in that time.

Once the trial started our visits galloped. It was like being an astronaut getting into the part of the prison where Mick and I could face one another through a wall of glass. Electronic wands had been whisked around me five or six times between the entrance and this inner sanctum. I stated my name and business like a parrot, I stood in three different passages with a door locked behind me before the one in front could unlock. I was always surprised not to be given a bullet-proof outfit at the last door. The building was new and clean, not like I would have imagined it. The corridors were wide and well lit; some had posters on the walls, others had high windows through which you could see a slit of sky above more walls. It was more like Heathrow Airport than a prison. And in the middle of all those tons of breeze blocks and concrete was Mick. We had an hour usually.

He was nervous on that Saturday. The prosecution were near the end of their case now and the defence would begin to present theirs next week.

'This is it now, Christy,' he said, leaning forwards to be close to me through the glass. 'It'll all be over soon now.'

'Is Maisie going to be called?' I didn't want to talk about when it was all over, it made me uncomfortable. The future was suspended for him like the rest of life. 'She wants to know because if she's not called she can come with me to court.'

He grinned and put his hands on the glass as if he were touching my face.

'She's way too sexy to have in the witness stand, she'd be a confusing sight for everyone, you know.'

I leapt back from the screen as if his hands had scorched me through it.

'If that's how you feel, get Maisie to come and see you every week. Get Maisie to run around after you and buy you clothes and batteries and make you tapes. Get her to stand up for you in pubs when people you don't even know bad-mouth you.' All the frustration was welling over now. I stood up, shaking, and turned to go.

Mick bashed on the glass like an ape at the zoo.

'Christy, sweetheart, I love you. Please come back.'

His shouting pain pulled me back to face him. The guards shuffled their feet, turned their faces to one side trying to merge with the walls. My mouth was bitter with rage and embarrassment, but I couldn't walk out of the door. I moved closer to the barrier; my breath smudged Mick's face, softening him. I wiped the glass clean again. I wanted to break it and hit him.

'Well, what did you mean then?'

He was almost crying and his scar was white as lint on his flushed forehead. Guilt crept across my anger. I had deliberately misunderstood him, of course he didn't fancy Maisie, he didn't even like her, but I had been sensible and capable for so long now. I wanted to sob and scream and have him console me. What use is a boyfriend if you can't even touch him? I sat down again and blew my nose.

He sat down too, big and defeated behind the screen.

'You can go if you want to, Christy. You know I can't stop you.'

A bell thudded through the walls. It was the end of the

visit. The guards stepped forward out of the walls, one to take me out and away, the other to lead Mick back to his cell.

Mick turned in his chair.

'Please, just a minute more.'

'All right, lad, but make it quick.' The guard on his side stepped back and nodded to the other one.

Mick's voice was low and urgent.

'Don't do all this from pity, Christy. I can handle this mess if you want to split, but I can't be helping you make decisions. Maisie doesn't need to be a witness. End of story. I was joking, having a laugh, you know that girl.' His voice wavered, he wasn't in control, he was almost pleading.

My anger swelled, but the guards came forward again and Mick stood to be handcuffed and led back to his cell. I didn't move until he had gone.

In my head I carried on arguing as I joined the halting queue of women leaving. Getting out took hours, even longer than getting in, or maybe it just felt longer. Driving away I relished the smooth acceleration of the car on a fast road. Mick and I didn't have momentum let alone acceleration. We were stagnant; each visit began with expectation and ended too soon, and every word we said to one another was overheard by guards. I had never been able to talk to him about the arrest or what he had done. We couldn't talk, we couldn't argue, we couldn't even kiss. Every time I went I decided to stop seeing him, but I couldn't do it. The news on the radio had a report about some hostages being released. I turned it off and cried for as long as it took to drive the ten miles home.

I wanted to have fun that night, and to be apart from anyone who knew Mick. I went to a pub in Lynton where people from the college gathered and I got drunk. When the pub closed a group of us went to someone's bedsit, I don't know whose. We made cocktails of Bacardi and milk which were disgusting. A boy with fair hair in a sweep down one side of his face came up to me. I recognised him. He was called Daley Jennings and he had been a bully in the year above me at school. He tried to kiss me without even saying hello. I ducked away from his wet mouth and his bad breath and locked myself in the bathroom. Sitting on the basin examining my hazy face, I was ashamed. If this is the best I can do on my own I can't criticise Mick. I've forgotten how to behave without him. I needed to be sick to be sober and to get home. Crouching by the lavatory I pushed my fingers too far down my throat till I retched. No one paid any attention when I left. Daley Jennings was asleep with his mouth open, folded double like a clothespeg across the bottom stair.

Christy lay in the bath. The water had cooled to match her blood so if she moved she could feel a line of warmth around her body as if she had drawn it with a red felt pen. In her mind Mick and Ben stood side by side, arms out straight like the cut-out dolls she had loved as a child. They were dressed. Ben wore a yellow T-shirt, a little shiny and a little too tight, and some blue-and-white-striped dungarees. He often wore dungarees. She put Mick in a navy cotton shirt and the nasty tracksuit she had once seen him wear. She shut her eyes for better concentration. This was good. Mick was handicapped by the tracksuit. She could now be objective. In her mind she wanted each of them to smile, and then say hello. She wanted to compare them for dependability. The Ben doll licked his lips before he smiled, and his chin sank into his neck above the gold chain Maisie had given him. Creepy, but then maybe he's shy, Christy thought, and moved over to the Mick doll. He looked straight at her and his smile was warmer than the bath. She lay in satin water until the bathroom turned grey around her, thinking of life with Mick and his dog Hotspur.

Later Christy and Danny went into Lynton to meet Mick. Danny was supposed to go and play pool with some friends, but somehow he didn't say goodbye in the pub where they met, and bought Coca-Cola for Mick and beer for himself, occasionally remembering Christy, until closing time. Christy liked sharing Mick with Danny. She slouched on the red banquette, trickling smoke up past her narrowed eyes.

'Come on, Christy, stir yourself, girl. Play pool with us.' Danny handed her a cue and a block of dusty chalk. 'Naylor versus Fleet and Naylor is a two-man team, OK?'

'Let's have a bet,' said Mick, and he pulled a fan of money from his pocket.

Christy could see the note he laid on the edge of the

pool table from the other side. It was foreign-looking, big and pink.

'You've got to bet English money,' she protested, and Mick picked it up and brought it round the table to her.

He was too close for her to see him properly; she stood back from him, bumping into the table with him still too big in front of her. He waved the money, fanning her nose, and his eyes were slits staring out of a stranger's face.

'It is English, sweetheart. It's a fifty.'

Christy's heart thumped.

'Don't be silly Mick, we can't match that. Why are you doing this? And why have you got all that money?'

Mick's face in the dim pub had shadows she didn't recognise.

'I took it out of the bank,' he said, and shutting the fan he ran his thumb across the corner. This whole stack, as thick as a pack of cards, was made up of fifty-pound notes.

'Why did you take out so much cash?' she whispered. His nail purred across the stiff paper, he knew she was angry and he laughed.

Mick tucked the money back into his jacket and grabbed Christy, hugging her hard and whirling her round off her feet so her shoe caught a table and another customer's calves.

'Because I can,' he said into her hair. 'I can take out as much as I want and there's still more when I go back.'

Danny came over.

'Come on, let's get this game up and running.' He saw Mick's money and raised his eyebrows. 'You're very sure of your skills,' he said. 'Christy and I will pay in kind if we lose, OK?'

'Not me,' said Christy, now white and hot.

'I don't play if I can't pay.'

Mick embraced her again.

'Come on, sweetheart, your presence is worth twice that for half an hour.'

Danny didn't seem worried about winning Mick's money. Christy sighed and picked up her pool cue again. Maybe it would all make sense later. She played the first shot. The game was over soon. Mick took too many risks, the balls spun and bumped and sometimes went in, he seemed to want to lose. Danny played slowly and set up his shots with care. Christy had hardly anything to do. When Mick handed her the fifty-pound note she couldn't look at him. Danny took it.

'Let's get some drinks.' He moved away to the bar.

Christy in her corner seat lost sight and sound of the surrounding crowd. Mick was all she could see. Mick and his money in the smoke-deep bar.

Driving with Danny back to Mick's house late, Mick's car flickering red lights far ahead, Christy was silent. Danny was not.

'It'll be great tomorrow. I'm going with Mick to buy a new car. That's what he had all that money for, you know. He told me not to say anything to you, but as you're so sulky I think you should know. Now will you pull yourself together?'

Christy rubbed her eyes and dug into her bag for cigarettes.

'I wonder why I wasn't supposed to know.'

Danny swung the car down the track towards the cottage, his thin hands tight on the wheel.

'It's obvious, Chris.' He spoke gently, as if he was the grown-up and Christy a child. 'He wants you to trust him and he saw that you didn't. He's probably upset. You should apologise.'

Danny was so certain, so sensible. Christy closed her eyes and saw herself like rot, gnawing away at Mick until he stopped being good and strong and fell to dust at her feet.

7

Danny should have been a girl. That's what Jessica said until he was six when suddenly he became her favourite because he was a boy and he could never outshine her. Maisie and Christy were becoming far too pretty far too soon. When Danny was small Jessica would not accept his maleness. She sidestepped his gun toting, dogged in her belief that she could change him by spreading before him a future strewn with flower presses and magic sets. But he turned sticks into guns and cardboard boxes into tanks, he took avid pleasure in squatting by flattened frogs and hedgehogs on the road. He put them in his flower press.

Jessica had no brothers nor indeed sisters herself and had fallen in love with Frank because he was gentle, and not like the barking red-faced youths her parents had encouraged her to meet at shooting parties and on skiing trips. Her life now was as neat and feminine as the floral wallpaper she had hung in her living room, except for the presence of Danny. By the time he was six she knew she could not steer him, and instead she changed her own course. She was fascinated by the man she could see Danny would become. His maleness ceased to be a threat and became an obsession.

She had schooled Frank and bent him to her will, their lives ran as she wished them to and he complied. Danny was different. He played with her. He flirted with her. When he wanted her to let him go to a football match with Frank he didn't argue his point. He just looked at her. She could not resist him. She always gave in with Danny. She admired him for opposing her and for his pleasure in getting away with it.

Frank remonstrated.

'You can't have one rule for the girls and another for Danny; it isn't fair on any of them.'

Jessica tossed her head.

'I don't. Anyway, the girls are older, they should know better by now.'

And despite her inconsistencies, Jessica's children loved her, she was sure. Jessica was thirty-five when she looked in the mirror one morning and knew she wanted more.

Mick wandered along a shingle path and stopped, facing away from Christy. He never came too close when they visited Jessica's grave, and he didn't speak until they were back in the car again driving out past terraced houses and the liquorice lines of the railway track. It was the new car. Christy couldn't see how it was different from the old car, but Danny and Mick had both told her it was perfect. The best car around for now.

'I'm going away tomorrow for a few days, and I asked Danny if he'd be wanting to go with me.' He stopped at traffic lights and rested his hand on Christy's knee.

She looked away, excluded, repulsed by his bitten fingernails.

'You never take me,' she said.

'It's not your sort of thing, Christy, and anyway, you're working. He's going to help me do some research. We're going to Reading. I've got some people to see there.'

She wanted to know who he was seeing, why he needed

a new car, why he never took her with him, but she didn't ask. It was better to glide on the surface, darting between these half-submerged questions without touching them. The leaping joy of being with him, of having a boyfriend, had steadied. There were parts of him she didn't know, places where she couldn't reach him. He was attentive and thoughtful, he gave her presents and bought her dinner whenever they went out. He wanted her with him in his house and he was dependable. But Christy wanted more. She became captious and determined to see into his soul. But by now she knew if she asked too many questions he would close himself off for days, leaving her scrambling in confusion. He loved her, he hadn't said so but he would soon, and this fuelled her crusade. In time he would be open, quite open. As she was with him.

They took Hotspur to the sea and walked along the ragged shore beneath the stony bulge of the sea defences. Above them cliffs crumbled soft sugar brown and Hotspur dashed up, pausing then hurling himself back down to the sea. Pebbles round and tight like roe shored up in hills and valleys along the wide beach and in the distance their smoky purple met the sea beneath a ribbon of foam. September sun crept in and out of fleeting cloud casting bruises on to the sea. Mick flicked stones into the water sending Hotspur into a spin of hysterical pleasure. His face was sleek and wet like an otter and he panted at Mick's side, barking and leaping to and fro but determined not to set foot in the sea. Christy sat behind them on banked stones, her arms clasped around her knees and her face turned up to the sun.

Mick threw a last flint for the dog and knelt down beside her.

'A seashore for your thoughts,' he said smiling, balancing two round pebbles on her knees.

'I was thinking about you, wondering about your family.' If she didn't ask a direct question she might catch him out.

Mick lay flat beside her and closed his eyes, his scar a fine colourless ridge like a hook caught beneath his skin.

'We never had anything like you've got, Christy. My dad worked in a brewery and Ma was a nurse in an old people's home. They've retired now, and there's no money. They were never there when we came back from school, and it didn't take us long to realise that they would never know if we didn't go to school at all. None of my mates went anyway. There wasn't much to do during the day there, so we used to nick cars and bikes, anything to get you out of that place, even for half an hour.'

They lay side by side, feet towards the sea, listening to waves crashing on stones. Christy shaded her eyes and looked up at no-colour sky. Autumn sharpened the air and stretched shadows down over the sea scent of salt and wet sand. Danny was going back to college next week. Maisie was already in the latest look for the new season, her tan scrubbed off, her hair pinned high and tight like a Victorian governess. Christy twisted to look at Mick. He had placed two pebbles in the sockets of his eyes and straightened himself as if he had been marked and discarded by the sea.

'Don't. You look dead, Mick.'

She took the stones off his face and pulled him up. She couldn't bear to think of him filling his childhood with petty crimes and danger; she wanted to make it all right, she wanted it not to have happened like that.

'Is your sister still living there?'

'Yeah, she works in a day-care centre, and at night she goes home to Ma and Da and cooks for them. She's older than me, five years older. I don't think she'll get out now.'

Hotspur bounced towards them from the sea, his mouth

full, the hairs on his chin dripping in a goatee beard. He came closer and Christy saw that the beard had claws, wildly twitching then falling still for a moment.

'He's got a crab. God, he's disgusting.' She got up and called the dog.

He came to her, eyes bright with pride, tail spinning. The crab waved at her, Hotspur dropped it and barked a challenge, stretching down on his front legs, enjoying the game. On the ground the crab pulled itself together like a puppet ready for action. Christy suddenly couldn't pick it up. The grey-blue shell gleamed and the claws snapped. She pushed it with her toe and the sea caught it, whirling it to and fro until it vanished beneath a slapping wave.

She turned back to Mick. He was sitting up, his arms loose and long at his side. He grabbed her hand and pulled her down next to him.

'Christy the emancipator. You're too kind-hearted, sweetheart, you'll never get through unless you toughen up, now, will you?'

She giggled and lay back against his shoulder.

'I'm not. I just don't like seeing a disadvantaged crab. If you were caught in someone's mouth I'd get you out as well.'

He rolled over on top of her, pinning her flat on the cobbled surface, holding her tighter, tighter.

'I love you, Christy.'

He'd said it now.

This time when Mick was away, Christy wanted to go out. Bolstered by mutually declared love she shed her skin of transparent shyness and swam out supple and strong, gleaming beauty and confidence in every gesture. At the trout farm the fishing was slowing down now the days were not so warm, but there were still restaurant orders to fill, and the smoke house was sulking. Everything came out scorched. Christy's clothes were pungent with the salt-dry smell of oversmoked fish, her hair frizzed from too much time spent leaning into the oven, and she was convinced that her face was beginning to take on the leathered sheen of dried fish skin.

Frank gave her the weekend off and she caught the little train into Lynton. The two short carriages filled up as the train paused at village stations and clusters of women in tight shoes crowded on, their wrists creased around the handles of too many deflated shopping bags. Fields marooning church towers gave way to car-parks and net-curtained windows as the train drifted into Lynton. Leaning too far out of the window, Christy watched the spaghetti chaos of rail tracks unravel until three strands remained and she was too close to see them run up to the platforms and stop.

Maisie's hairdressing salon was in the centre of town, near the fountain where she and Christy had spent aimless hours as teenagers, swapping insults with boys they half knew as a prelude to being snogged by them in the station waiting room. As Christy walked by she noticed a row of girls giggling, sitting on the wall around the fountain, their feet obscured by piles of plastic bags full of cheap dresses bought this morning at Dorothy Perkins for the party tonight. Relentless, unchanging Saturday behaviour: Christy was depressed by the sameness of it. Two youths, crew-cut and dressed in shapeless dirty jackets and trainers, sat down near the girls, lit cigarettes and began to swap loud remarks about the slappers they had been with last night. She turned away, not wanting to see the girls toss their hair and beckon with shining eyes and gestures until the youths sidled close to them and the insults began. She suddenly wished Frank had taken her further away when

Jessica died, to a new town where experience could start again. But then she would never have met Mick. Mick could take her away. They could live in London maybe, or in a little cottage with gingham curtains. He could do that kind of thing, he was free. He could give her his life to share. There was nothing to tie him to anyone but her.

Wrapped in fantasy, Christy entered Maisie's salon. Music pumped over the whir of hairdriers. Maisie winked at her but went on parting and combing wet white hair on the head of a friend of Jessica's. All Jessica's friends came to the salon where Maisie worked, and they all requested Maisie. With them came a trail of quiet tweed and pleats, button-down shirts and shiny handbags to match the shoes. Jessica had never looked like them, never been one of them, but they were fond of her and determined to help still, three years on. They weren't comfortable in this setting of chrome, bright lights and big music. They had to submit to having their hair washed in sinks shaped like dog bowls and the mirrors had atrophied snakes and spears twisted in the frames, but they came for Jessica's sake. They must support her daughter, it was all that could be done.

Maisie was furious.

'God, I've got bloody Marjory Perkins and then Elizabeth Moore today,' she whispered to Christy when the white-haired chairwoman of the WI had gone, leaving a small tip and a faint aroma of talcum-powdered goodness behind her. Maisie washed brushes vigorously and carried on. 'They all ask for me and I spend my whole time doing sets and rinses. I can't stand it, I never have time to do anyone young, and those old bags just go on and on about poor dear Jessica and poor dear Frank, was it wise for him to start that trout farm, until I want to chop their stupid tongues off, or at least give them peroxide instead of brunette rinse.'

'Well, you can do me if you like,' Christy offered, 'but don't cut too much off. I don't want it to look any shorter, or any different.'

Maisie threw her scissors and combs into a tall jar of blue liquid and wiped her hands on her skirt.

'No bloody thanks, but I'll meet you for a drink after work. Why are you here anyway?'

Typical Maisie, thought Christy. I don't know why I go on trying to please her.

'I'm coming to stay with you tonight. I thought we could go out and have fun. We haven't been on our own for ages.'

Maisie was delighted.

'Is Mick away? Oh good. We can go to a party or something and get really dolled up. It's Anna's hen night; she won't mind if you come. I'm sick of bloody boyfriends after Ben being back here for all that time. You should see the state of the flat. He's bought another motor bike, or some bits of one anyway. He's a right pain and he wouldn't take me to London when I asked him to.'

A discreet cough interrupted her and the broad figure of Marjory Perkins loomed in the mirror, or as much of her as would fit. The sensible shoes and broad calves were cut off by the table, and the beige mackintosh sleeves, one dangling a handbag, the other caught tight by the hook of her umbrella, were set too far apart on either side of her solid frame to be seen in the mirror.

'Hello, my dear, I'm so glad you had an appointment for me. Alan has a directors' dinner this evening, and I haven't had a moment to see poor Frank since I don't know when . . .'

Maisie pushed her down into the chair and engulfed the kindly tinkle of her conversation in a white towel.

'God save me,' she whispered, rolling her eyes.

Christy laughed and left the salon. She wanted to buy a present for Mick. It was his birthday on Hallowe'en; six weeks away but she was determined to have everything organised well in advance. She thought she might give him a surprise party at the cottage, his present would be bestowed beforehand in the morning, if only she could find the right thing.

The new shopping mall with its piped music and warm air was a good place to start. Christy joined the trail of slow-moving shoppers at the entrance and with them began to wander through the arcades. It was like being under water; all sound was softened and dulled and the faces turned towards shop windows were expressionless and pale green, reflecting the glass roof and the mossy carpeting. She realised she had been standing in front of a men's clothes shop for five minutes without taking anything in. The clump of shoppers she had come in with had moved on through the hall. She could see the red anoraks of one couple bobbing back and forth in a shoe shop. She watched the two bending and rising then stopping as they tied laces and looked at one another's feet, incongruous in pristine shoes beneath old jeans. In a minute they would sail out again and on, extra plastic bags banging against their calves.

Christy suddenly didn't want to buy Mick something big. It had to be small, not heavy but visibly expensive, something she could slip into her pocket, or into his when she gave it to him at breakfast on his birthday. She wandered into an electrical shop, past a bank of televisions like windows in a tower block, busy and unheeding of their neighbours but displaying uniform scenes in lurid colours. Green turf on a smaller television at the side attracted her and she watched a race start, the horses breaking in kaleidoscope pattern as the flag went up, then reforming in a long tight chain as they

104

found their positions as near to the front and as close to the railings as they could manage. The jockeys perched above their backs like harlequins in a parade, still and faceless as the horses hurtled towards the final straight. The front runner was drawing ahead now, its body lengthening, the muscles standing out on its quarters so it seemed to be pulling the others behind it on an invisible string. A few people then a mass came into view at the railings and the horse slowed as it passed the post. Christy wasn't watching the race though; she crouched by the screen, willing the camera to move back from the winner whose jockey was punching the air in victory. She had seen Mick. It must have been him, tall and dark with his long black coat on, standing beside the finish. Her heart bumped in her chest as though she had caught him in bed with someone. Maybe it wasn't him. It couldn't be. The camera was slow, so slow to move back to the course. There was no sound, she didn't know where the race was, she didn't know if they would show it again.

The picture changed; it was the track and the horses again. Second and third place were decided by a photo finish. The finishing post jerked into view, the mass of green and brown and blue jackets behind the white railings appeared as they had before. She knelt in front of the television trying not to blink, searching the shunting picture for Mick, but the black coat wasn't there. She thought she saw it moving back in the crowd, but her eyes were hot with staring and she wasn't sure. The picture changed again, a different race in progress, a different track. She could tell because the railings were curved at the top. Pink and stiff with embarrassment and fury, she stood up and walked out of the shop without looking at the staff, afraid that they were watching her and knew she had seen her boyfriend where he hadn't said he would be.

*　　*　　*

Christy only told Maisie because she knew Maisie would dismiss it. They were getting ready to go out, clothes washed up around the bed where Maisie lay painting her fingernails.

'What a bastard,' said Maisie. 'He's probably got another girlfriend and a few children you don't know about. You shouldn't let him get away with it, Chris.'

Cold like a river streamed through Christy. 'You mean you think I did see him? You don't think it was a mistake? Maybe it was someone else who looks like him. It's not likely to be him, is it?'

If she hadn't told Maisie she could have forgotten it, pretended she'd imagined it. She would never have mentioned it to Mick because he would think she was so crazy about him she'd started seeing things. Maisie was meant to back her up and say she was daft. But Maisie knew it was Mick. She hadn't even questioned it. She accepted it and moved on to her toenails.

It must have been him. She must ask him. She would die if she didn't ask him now, this minute.

Maisie stood up, splaying her toes, and waddled across to Christy.

'You can't have him taking you for a ride like this. You've got to talk to him, get some explanations. Treat him mean, Christy, or you'll be trampled.' She patted Christy's back and kissed the top of her head.

Christy pressed her palms against her eyes, heaving breaths, not crying, please God, not crying.

The party was upstairs in a pub. Anna was an old friend of Maisie's from school; Christy had met her often before and liked her. Her round face was framed by candyfloss hair and her voice fluted like a child's. Christy thought it was a

106

shame she was getting married, it would encourage Maisie. Christy had never been to a hen night before. She didn't know anyone who was married, apart from proper adults. Maisie was engaged, of course, but that was different. Christy didn't believe that Maisie and Ben would ever get married. Maisie liked being engaged for the same reasons that she liked the motor bike in her flat: it gave her a reputation, it made her different.

Anna, though, was serious about her forthcoming nuptials, and kissing Maisie when she arrived, announced that she was determined to enjoy the hen night to the death. Not a detail had been forgotten. The girls giggled and squealed with faked pleasure when the phallic-shaped menus were brought. The green drinks they sipped were called Screaming Orgasms, and the food was served by three muscle-bound boys wearing shorts and vests. Christy's nerves jangled. She could not look at the other girls; she was trapped in her own thoughts, scrabbling round and round after Mick. She resented their noise, their laughter, their intrusions on her separateness. The longer she sat there, the more separate she became. She felt an icy disgust when Maisie, drunk, started stroking the waiters' arms when they leant over to serve her. The girl next to Christy was small and dark. She didn't drink and she pushed her food around her plate, eating only the salad when it arrived limp and wan after its voyage from the kitchens.

Christy caught her eye and smiled; the girl stared back at her.

'How do you know Anna?' Time would pass more quickly if she talked.

'I massage her, I'm learning aromatherapy. You're Mick Fleet's girlfriend, aren't you? I've done him as well.'

Christy looked at the girl's hands. They were small;

long nails yellow and repulsive flicked crumbs across the tablecloth. Christy shivered imagining those hands on Mick's back. She pretended she knew.

'Oh yes, I remember Mick saying he liked aromatherapy, I've never had it . . .' Her voice trailed off, she was stuck, she couldn't think of anything else to say. She wished she had never started talking to this girl. 'What's your name?'

'Linda. You're Christy, aren't you? Mick talks about you sometimes.'

Talks not talked. Christy lit a cigarette, letting her hair fall over her face to give herself time. Another waiter came in and whispered to Anna at the top of the table; she nodded and music poured into the room. Everyone looked up, their mouths open. Anna giggled, straightening in her seat and pushing her hair back. The waiter began swaying and as he swayed he fumbled with the buttons of his shirt. His face was in shadow, a tear of sweat wobbled on his cheek. He brushed it off, keeping his eyes on Anna as he dragged off his shirt. A stripper. Christy felt sorry for him. She wondered if he was drunk, or if he did this night after night for hot-skinned half-cut girls, protected from them by his own glass bowl of stony sobriety. He wasn't even good-looking. His clothes drooped and fell to the floor; he couldn't muster the panache to fling them across the room in the traditional manner. Inch by inch his body emerged, stodgy and much too hairy. Linda suddenly pushed her plate into the centre of the table, knocking her glass over and Christy's next to it. Red wine swelled then sank into the pink cloth. Christy thought about mopping it up but couldn't be bothered.

Linda was leaning forwards across the table towards Anna, her hands spreading in the spongy cloth, yellow nails flexing.

'How could you do this, Anna? It's grotesque. Who's enjoying it? Anyone?' She looked round at the over-made-up girls, each one looked away, not wanting to meet her eyes.

Maisie rose and glared down at Linda. The stripper carried on undressing, slowly, halfheartedly. Maisie drank her wine before she spoke, a good gesture as it gave everyone time to focus on her.

'I think you should go, Linda. You're upsetting Anna.'

Christy had been tensed for Maisie to shout and rant, to start tearing her own clothes off to prove her point. But she was quiet and in control; Linda seemed the fool, not the stripper, not even the gawping girls. Not Maisie. Christy relaxed and inhaled pride at her sister diffusing awkwardness instead of intensifying it. Linda picked up her bag and rushed out of the room, her long scarf trailing with pathetic flamboyance behind her. Christy hoped she was crying. Her drunkenness vanished, Maisie knelt next to Anna, making her laugh, and the girls next to her, until the whole table had unfrozen again.

Walking home to the flat with Maisie, Christy's step was jaunty with admiration for her sister and satisfaction at the downfall of Linda.

'You were brilliant, Maisie, you saved Anna from a miserable night. I don't know what made Linda do that. She wasn't even drinking.' They were passing Maisie's salon now. Christy looked in and stopped dead. A huge photograph filled the window. 'My God, Maisie. Look at this.' Maisie laughing looked out at Maisie laughing looking in and Christy next to her, dwarfed by her giant black-and-white sister.

'They put it up this afternoon; it only arrived from the enlargement place yesterday. What do you think?'

Christy didn't know what she thought. It was the picture

Mick had taken the first time he met Maisie and Danny. The handle bars of the motor bike curved gleaming chrome; Christy remembered Maisie leaning forwards between them led on by Mick's flow of sweet talk. She turned away, cold suddenly; Maisie had moved on.

'I didn't know you were using that picture for the shop.' She hurried after Maisie along the street. 'I didn't know you even had that picture.'

'Mick sent it the other day and they needed something big so they enlarged it.' Maisie was unconcerned, feeling in her bag for keys as they turned down towards her building. 'It's good, isn't it?'

Christy nodded.

'It's very good. I wish you'd told me.'

Maisie sighed.

'It's no big deal, Chris. You should stop getting so wound up about things.'

In the flat Maisie went into the bathroom to brush her teeth. Christy leaned in the doorway of the sitting room. Orange light flooded in from the street and danced on the motor bike, sending warped shadows across the floorboards. The air was warm and smelt of stale scent; Christy's face sagged with exhaustion. There were questions knocking somewhere in her mind but sleep shrouded them and she couldn't think. Something wrong was happening and her body could not face it. She got into Maisie's scrambled bed and shut her eyes. Maisie came through moments later: Christy was already asleep, fully dressed with her heels prodding the blankets. She looked like a small child in dressing-up clothes. Maisie took the shoes off and got in beside her. She wished Jessica could tell her how to help Christy.

Maisie was late. I heard her rattle in through the main doors of the court house even though I was halfway up the second flight of stairs. Her bracelets clanked as she heaped them on the table beside the metal detector and her voice carried up through the hall. 'Do you have to empty my bag? Those are nail scissors. Are they really offensive? Oh, I see, you think I might stab someone with them. Well, I'll collect them from you later, shall I?' Then her heels sharp across the floor and there she was in a cloud of scent and clean hair, wearing her pink fake-fur coat and hardly any skirt. 'Sorry I'm late. Have we missed it?' She followed me through to the next checkpoint, giggling. 'It's just like the Great Escape, isn't it?'

We entered the courtroom. Tobin was standing, one elbow on his little folding table, the other draped in his black gown. He lost where he was in one of those endless sentences as his eyes bulged over Maisie, forcing silence into the room while we shuffled along to a pair of free seats in the public gallery. Mick hardly looked up, but the black-haired boy in the jury pushed his fingers through his hair and straightened his shoulders; next to him Lemon Face pursed her lips. Even the Judge gazed at Maisie, his eyebrows peaking to graze his wig.

Tobin took off his spectacles and wiped them on an ostentatious handkerchief. He shook it out and starched folds made a pattern of criss-cross shadow on white linen. He really strung this sort of thing out. To him the courtroom was a stadium. I'd seen him during lunch breaks talking to Mick's barrister, sucking on a cigar at the pub they all went to, and there he merged into his chair and his surroundings, a pompous figure always, but not posturing the way he did in court. He knew the value of body language as well as a rock star. He put his spectacles back on and began to rev his speech up again. He had a policeman in the witness box and he was on his way to a major revelation. I could tell now when Tobin felt on top of things. He stood tall, swaying back and forth in the tiny space he filled between his desk and the one behind; if he'd been at home he would be pacing around his drawing room swilling brandy in a big glass.

'Exhibit 85, please.' He looked over his spectacles at the clerk who shuffled out, allowing Tobin several seconds to gaze at Maisie. His side-kick nudged him and he leant down to receive instructions, his eyes never leaving Maisie's face.

The clerk reappeared in front of two policemen. They were carrying a bulky polythene parcel sealed with yellow tape.

'What's that?' Maisie whispered, but I shook my head.

'Don't know. It looks like a set of drainrods to me.'

Tobin's voice was plum deep in pleasure.

'Constable Rayne, do you recognise this exhibit?' The clerk was unwrapping the parcel on the table beneath the Judge's platform; the Judge slid forward on his throne to see. 'Your Honour, members of the jury, this exhibit was found in the grounds of Mr Fleet's house. Buried there, as Constable Rayne will tell us.'

Then he was off on those interminable questions, sifting every grain of nuance out of the policeman's responses until a dust of possibility lay over even the most insignificant yes or no.

'Would you tell the jury how you came to find the exhibit?'

'Can you show us on the plan of the property, which the jury will find on page seventeen of the third bundle, where precisely the exhibit was located?'

'Were you alone when you unearthed the exhibit?'

All the time he was asking, the policeman and the rest

of us in the courtroom had our eyes fixed on the exhibit as the clerk unwrapped whatever it was. It was like pass the parcel. A question, another layer, an answer, another layer. Even the Crown Jewels couldn't need that much padding. Tobin knew it would take ages. That was why he had asked if the policeman recognised it without waiting for an answer and before it was opened. He wanted everyone to be on tenterhooks.

Maisie was like a spaniel on a scent at my side; she didn't move, but her hair shivered down her cheek. The final yellow tape crunched through the silent room and there they were. Three guns. One sleek and black, slender as the drainrod I wished it had been, the other two maimed, cut short where the barrels were meant to be. I bit my tongue to stop my teeth shaking. Dad had a shotgun for rabbits and the occasional duck, but it was small, cartoon-like in its simplicity. These guns had big straps and sights and a menace which exploded in the courtroom like a shot.

This was one of Tobin's finest moments. No one moved but the air became stultifying, as if everyone had inhaled all the oxygen at once.

'Did these guns bear fingerprints, Constable Rayne?'

'Yes, sir, they did, sir.'

'And did these fingerprints tally with those given by the defendant to the police at the time of his arrest?'

I could only see the policeman's square back, flesh in a roll above his collar and then his hair.

'Yes, sir, they did.'

Triumph sleeked around Tobin like ermine.

'I have no further questions for this witness, Your Honour.'

I couldn't look at Mick. I didn't want to see his expression;

whatever it was it would be the wrong one for being accused of hiding guns.

Maisie squeezed my arm.

'Are you OK, Chris?' she whispered.

I nodded.

'Yes, I wish we could go out, though, but it would look bad, we'll have to hang on until the lunch break.'

Having peaked, Tobin threw himself into his chair and crossed his legs, ready to enjoy the defence cross examination. The headlines in the local paper the next day were robbed of absolute sensation by the fact that the Judge had ordered that Mick should not be named.

8

For a long time knowing there could be more was enough for Jessica. She created a world she could visit in her head without danger. Her made-up man was taciturn and tall. He wore a black coat and wrapped her in it with him. He cupped his hands around her head and looked into her eyes. She called him up when she was alone in the house, making beds or dusting. A housewife's fantasy. Part of her was ashamed, but she needed it. Daily routine was well worn now, with all three children at secondary school. She had always had Thursdays to herself: Frank had insisted she had one day of freedom. She had never done much with those Thursdays except walk. Along the beach with her pugs.

There had been a man, David, long ago, whom she had met one winter on the blank coastline. Her fantasies were based on him. They had walked and talked, never arranging to meet, but he was always there on Thursdays at ten in the morning. A small café hung over the cliffs at Oldsands, the windows clouded with salt spray on the outside and condensation on the inside. Jessica and David faced one another at a yellow formica table and drank dark tea; outside the pugs whined, glum patience setting their squashed faces. Jessica never felt she was doing anything wrong by meeting David. They were chaperoned by the po-faced presence of the three sisters who ran the café. The youngest one never smiled and had gypsy earrings and a shock of tobacco-yellow hair frizzed to wire by the sea wind. The other two were even less friendly, less colourful and less active. They sat knitting at a table near the gas heater, beneath a model lifeboat. Slowly, from their brief conversations as they passed her milk and took her money, Jessica learnt that they were fishermen's widows, all three of them, and they ran their café and knitted oil-wool jerseys for those who had survived their husbands on the treacherous North Sea.

David was a painter, and although neither of them mentioned their families, Jessica guessed that like her he was married and had children. They talked about art, they talked about the sea and the places they had grown up in. They never touched one another, not even an accidental brush of hands across the teacups, and they never discussed the future. One Thursday David didn't turn up, and Jessica never saw him again. Except in her imagination.

It was much later that she embarked upon a real affair. She blamed Frank. He forced her into it, she told Vaughan, who leaned her chin into her glass and nodded, breathless in her need to hear more. Frank thought she should get a job, something to take her away from the house. He suggested it to staunch the flow of discontent she had begun to wallow in. He meant well. Jessica found a job in an antique shop in Lynton, and at first all went according to plan. The owner was an acquaintance of Frank's and had sold an antique dinner service for Jessica. It was the perfect place for her to work, surrounded by relics of a past similar to her own. The smell of beeswax and lavender reminded her of childhood, and she loved the three mornings she spent each week in the shop. Charlie Clement, the owner, was so civilised, so open to her suggestions of displays and repainting. Home began to look cheap and suburban.

'Well, it is suburban,' Frank pointed out. 'We live in a suburb. What do you expect?'

Jessica's discontent welled again.

Charlie lived alone in Lynton's New Town in a square Georgian house. He was tall and broad, his face and his too-long hair fitted her fantasy and he drove around in a gun-dark Jaguar with leather seats, a box of cigars within arm's reach. He was in love with Jessica before she came to work for him. He had been since the day he bought her aunt's dinner service from her at a price he could never sell it on for.

Jessica's mornings in the shop spilled into afternoons when Charlie began taking her out to lunch. This time she knew she was doing something wrong, but she didn't care. He was interested in her, he offered luxury and calm. At home the girls and Danny had become teenagers and she railed and screamed at them for their door-slamming, secret-smoking, bathroom-based existence. Frank was never there. He didn't buy her flowers. Charlie gave her long-stemmed roses to go on her desk, a watch because she didn't have one. A succession of trinkets from him crept into her handbag. She couldn't take them out; Frank would know where they came from.

He knew she was having an affair. He said nothing, but his eyes following her around the kitchen as she made supper pleaded with her. She pretended not to notice. Charlie wanted her to leave Frank and come away with him. She began to feel suffocated. Both of them were importuning her, their methods as diverse as their personalities, and, she thought wryly, their motives. Frank continued silent supplication, fear of her leaving gagging him until he scarcely spoke at all. Charlie talked ceaselessly, his intention to wear her defences down until she was swept away with him. It was like the Chinese water torture. She was confused and claustrophobic, unhappy with either of them, unable to imagine life without both. How could she make such a choice? Why could things not continue as they were? She thought she would go insane. Instead she got cancer.

They were back. Danny returned home late one night, dropped off by Mick who didn't come in.

Danny threw his bag down in the hall and headed for the fridge.

'God, I'm starving. I haven't had a decent meal for days.'

He was unkempt and high with excitement; Christy in her dressing gown couldn't get any sense out of him.

'What have you been doing then? Surely you could buy food, couldn't you?'

Danny laughed, spreading mustard thick on sliced bread, eating half the ham before it reached the sandwich. The microwave flashed green in the corner, its rhythm in tune with the tick of Jessica's old kitchen clock. Danny put the kettle on, throwing teabags into mugs he found dirty in the sink. His hair was matted like a baby's at the back; at the front it wedged behind his ears and appeared to have grown shaggy and much longer in his few days' absence.

'You wouldn't believe it, Chris. You just wouldn't believe what fun we've had,' he kept repeating.

'Well, tell me, for God's sake, or else shut up.' Christy was tired and irritated; he was behaving as if she wasn't there, slamming round the kitchen dropping crumbs and making a mess.

She found herself trailing behind him, a cloth poised to mop every surface he touched. As they passed the sink in their odd formation dance she threw the cloth down.

'No, I'm not doing it. Danny, make sure you leave the kitchen tidy. And please tell me what you and Mick did tomorrow.'

She turned the main light in the kitchen off as she went out, leaving Danny humming to himself and opening cupboards in the Martian half-light of the microwave. It was almost dawn when she heard him going to his room.

Danny slept half the next day and then stayed in his room packing for college. He wouldn't talk to Christy or Frank; he just whistled and turned up the radio when they went into the room.

Mick rang early in the evening. Christy listened to him pouring out blandishments with a sour expression on her face.

'Sweetheart, I've missed you. I want to see you now. When do you finish work? I'll pick you up and take you somewhere special.'

'No, don't pick me up. I'll come to you at about seven. See you then.'

She put the phone down, a wave of savage pleasure rushing through her because Mick was still talking when the line went dead. It was better to be in control to see him, and she needed to be able to drive herself away after the confrontation.

The hours crawled. A truck arrived with one hundred nine-inch trout. Christy helped haul buckets from the tank to the water's edge and heave the slithering fish into the lake. The surface bubbled and churned, opaque and uninviting, and the smell of pond weed and sticky trout hung at the back of Christy's throat making her want to gag. Three men and Christy emptied the huge tank, ladling stunned trout into buckets then immersing the fish in the shallows and waiting a second while they swayed in their plastic cavern before flicking ribbed tails and gliding, stately as long boats, into the depths of the water. Christy wondered if they explored the whole lake, following silk undulations of mud into every depth and shallow, or if they took their freedom for granted and remained within a few feet of the edge, complacent in the knowledge that there was space should they want to discover it. Dragging more and never endingly more fish to water, she thought her back might snap, the surface of the tank sank so slowly. She clenched her teeth and carried on, her mind empty of anything save determination.

Danny and Frank were going to Lynton that evening to meet Maisie at a Chinese restaurant for Danny's last supper before returning to college.

'Bring Mick and come along,' urged Frank. 'It's not often we're all together now.'

Christy was kneeling by the washing machine, sorting through damp socks and shirts for her tights which Danny had washed along with his clothes.

'I'll see what Mick wants to do.' She leant further into the machine so Frank couldn't see her face. 'I might come on my own,' she added casually.

The sun was low on the horizon as she drove to Mick's cottage and the sky blurred pink around it. Christy turned the music up loud in the van and slowed down as she passed a series of water meadows where the sunset filled the valley and always lifted her spirits. A few cows grazed at the far end, their black-and-white bulk standing out bright and clean against the blur of the hedgerow.

Something huge descending caught her eye on the other

side of the road and she slowed the van by a gap in the hedge and stared. A helicopter hung in the air as low as the green-gold branches on a nearby oak tree. She looked back over her shoulder and two more swooped over the hedge and veering crazily lined themselves up facing the first one in the small roadside field. Christy turned off her music and the car engine and opened the window. Her hair billowed and whipped across her face as the blades of the three helicopters drummed up a mini cyclone. She was so close she could see the faces of the men in the cabins turned towards her. For a second she was terrified. I saw them so they'll have to kill me. They've been sent to kill me. They're going to machine gun my car. She wound up her window and the roar dulled a little. They increased their throttle power and their engines whined as they began to move. Christy couldn't drive on; she was part of this scene, the only spectator.

Like giant dragon-flies above a pond the helicopters darted back and forth between one another above the swirling grass, their camouflage turned to green and silver scales by the sun. Their unwieldy bloated forms assumed weightless grace as they dipped and turned, curtseying beneath their whirring blades. Then one by one they turned their tails in to the centre of the group and departed in different directions, still low as they sped away across fields until they were blobs, angry and black on the skyline. Christy was left alone again on the road, adrenalin surging, grinning insanely in a state of breathless excitement.

The front door of Mick's cottage was open but access was barred by a large motor bike parked with its front wheel wedged against the step. Christy heard voices as she slid past it, creeping into the cottage with a childish desire to see them before they saw her. A leather jacket sprawled inside the door, the back swollen like the curve of a turtle shell. Christy couldn't resist planting her foot in the middle of it. The voices came from the kitchen. Another man was here with Mick and they spoke fast, Mick's accent stronger than she had heard it before, echoing the other man's voice so they gabbled in unfamiliar rhythms as if they were speaking a foreign language.

She knew she must not interrupt them and froze in the sitting room, one foot lifted for her next step. The kitchen door opened and a head appeared. Christy took in white-grey skin bound above and below by ginger stubble, an earring and an expression of malevolence before she swayed and lost balance, crashing to the floor with a squawk.

'Hey, Mick, c'm 'ere now, will you? There's some girl lyin' on your floor.'

Mick came through.

'It's OK, Lennie, it's my girlfriend. Hello, sweetheart, are you all right down there now?'

Lennie's black boots filled Christy's field of vision, cracked leather and mud spilling down into the floor so he was rooted near her face. She got up and standing made him even larger, black-leather trousers, black shirt absorbing the light and the space in Mick's living room, taking the air away from Christy and draping her in darkness. She moved closer to Mick, safer when his arm was around her.

'This is Lennie, he's an old friend from Ireland come to stay for a few days.' Mick squeezed Christy's shoulder, forcing her to smile and say something pleasant.

Christy wished she hadn't come. She could smell hostility from Lennie, seeping out like old beer and wet ashtrays as he flicked red-lashed eyes over her.

'I didn't know you were busy, Mick. You said we could do something this evening. I've got to go and meet Dad and the others in town, I just wanted to see you first, I've missed you.' All the wrong things were coming out of her mouth, Lennie was watching her like a snake and she wanted to go.

She pulled away from Mick, fumbling for her car keys in her bag. They weren't there. Flushing pink, she poured her make-up and her address book on to the table with the empty cigarette packets and redundant lighters which collected in the bottom of her bag until it broke and she bought a new one. Neither of the men spoke; Christy leant over the debris of her possessions with her back to the room, as exposed as if she were naked.

'Maybe you didn't bring them out of the car.'

Mick went out to look, Christy swept her arm across the table, netting everything back into her bag, rushing so she could go and not be alone in the room with Lennie. Something clinked in his hands.

'You'll be wanting these now, won't you, girl?'

She turned to face him; her keys glittering on their chain dangled from his forefinger.

'You should be taking more care of them, you don't know where they might go otherwise.'

'You took them out of my bag, didn't you?' Anger extinguished her fear and she grabbed the keys from him and strode out of the cottage. 'I've got them now.' Her voice wavered and when she reached the car she had to lean on it because her limbs were collapsing.

'Good girl.' Mick opened the driver's door for her then closed it again when he noticed her face. 'What's the matter, sweetheart? I can't take you out, I've got to catch up with Lennie tonight.'

The concern in his voice plucked away her self-control and she burst into tears. Shaking her head she pushed past him into the car and drove off, crashing the gears.

The plate-glass windows of the Chinese restaurant were a pink smear of condensation and silk lanterns when Christy arrived. Frank, Maisie and Danny had started eating. Christy made for the lavatory before they saw her and in the green-tiled Ladies' she patted away her blotches and tears on a damp roller towel and feathered new mascara on to her eyelashes.

Maisie and Danny sat facing one another arguing. Frank leaning back on his chair discussed racing with the waiter, oblivious to the congealing rice in his bowl; none of them looked up when Christy joined them. She read the menu glancing sideways at her family, a smile creeping on to her face as she realised she was enjoying her invisibility because it meant she was a part of them. If Mick had come their entrance would have been so different: people always noticed him and were drawn to him. Christy teased him about it; she said he had animal magnetism. She liked the phrase without really knowing what it meant.

Danny had noticed her; he turned to her in appeal.

'Chris, Maisie can't see what I'm talking about, but I'm sure you will.'

Christy ate a prawn cracker, tipping her head back to expose her neck, long and pale, soft like the underbelly of a fish.

Danny grabbed her arm to make her listen.

'I was telling Maisie about these bikers I met with Mick. They were great guys, well, some of them. I thought she'd be interested as she and Ben have got that heap of rusting metal, but she says they're all wasters.'

'Well, they're not quite the same as Ben, are they?' Christy took some of her father's rice, waving her chopsticks with the grace of a conductor at a poignant stage of a performance.

Maisie laughed.

'No, they are not,' she said. 'A bunch of hairy hooligans. You shouldn't get mixed up with them, Danny.'

Danny banged the table.

'I'm not mixed up, I just said they could come and look me up when I'm back at college.'

Frank pointed his forefinger at Danny.

'You're teasing your sisters, and doing yourself no good, my boy. You think you can mess around with these people, but you can't.'

Masie interrupted.

'You are a student, you know. Not a character in a road movie.'

Danny pushed his chair back.

'God, you're so narrow-minded. Anyway, I was with Mick all the time, and he can tell good from bad. He liked them.'

The waiter arrived with a slithering mountain of noodles and Frank changed the conversation; he was glad Danny was returning to college the next day. Christy added a description of the helicopters she had seen, building her story up to mask her resentment. Danny seemed to have a better relationship with Mick than she did now.

Danny departed to college taking with him a small black kitten provided by Bloater the trout-farm cat. Christy cleaned his bedroom, mowing a path through the dust which had gathered over the summer. The dart board next to the window fell down when she brushed past it. Swearing under her breath, Christy bent to pick up the papers Danny had pinned to it. Among the litter of train tickets and cut-out football reports she noticed some money, a fifty-pound note. It was scribbled on in biro and craning towards the window she read the message: 'Keep this to remind you of salad days.'

It was written in square blue capitals. Christy poured over it, turning the note over and over hoping for further clues. She was curious, recalling Danny's conversation of the evening before. Maybe the bikers had done some drug deal with him. Christy was angry with herself for thinking such a thing. Danny wasn't interested in drugs, there must be another explanation. She finished cleaning the room, dusting and spraying the surfaces until the air reeked with the purging scent of polish.

At lunchtime she went out to the office, taking over from the girl who came to do book-keeping. From her window she saw brown billows from the smoke house. Frank was in there with a delivery of salmon. Christy hated the smoke house: its hot woody fug made her head ache; and she didn't like the withered flesh of smoked fish. She turned her chair so she was facing the main lake, a silver chalice in the grey autumn light, edged with copper trees; leaves drifted in wisps on the breeze. No one was fishing today and the lake was still save for a few ripples along the shore where some young moorhens swam, up-ending and vanishing and reappearing minutes later somewhere quite different. Christy doodled in her notebook, putting off the moment when she had to start writing an updated price list for restaurants.

The telephone rang. It was Mick.

'It's time we had some fun together, sweetheart. I'm going to take you to London, would you like to go on Wednesday?'

Swivelling her chair, Christy leaned over the desk, twisting her hair round her fingers, smiling at his nerve, his belief that she would jump when he said jump. And of course she did.

'I'd love that. We could stay with Aunt Vaughan. I'd like you to meet her.'

Mick was hardly listening.

'I can't see you till then, sweetheart. I'll be doing some business with Lennie and all that. You arrange things and make a list of what you want to buy. I want to give you a present for my birthday.'

'But it's not for ages.' Christy was surprised he mentioned it, even though she had been planning his present for a couple of weeks already.

His birthday was nearly a month away. She had written it in her diary in pink felt-tip the day he told her, embellishing the dot over the 'i' with a flower trailing hearts. She had quite wanted to un-write it when she was angry with him, especially as her diary was the one on the desk in the office and anyone could see it, but the pink pen was luminous and no amount of scribbling could hide her doting artwork.

'I know, but I think we could celebrate a bit in London. Who knows where we'll all be in a month's time. I'll be seeing you on Thursday then.' Mick was gone.

Christy knew she was never going to ask him if it had been him at the race meeting; she wasn't even going to ask him about being massaged by Linda. There was no need: he wanted to be with her, he was taking her to London.

She rang Aunt Vaughan and went to find Frank. He had stormed out in a fury earlier when Maisie telephoned to announce her plan to marry Ben in the spring. Christy was sceptical, Frank was not.

'She'll do it just to annoy me,' he complained, heading off to the smoke house with his sledge hammer.

Clad in an old boiler suit and his yellow building-site helmet, Frank looked like a coal miner when Christy found him in a crack between the smoke house and the garage it abutted. He was wedging bricks using mechanical sideways movements because there was no space for him to bend forwards. He was also wedged and Christy laughed so much she could hardly hear him.

'Thank God you've come, Chris. I got the sledge hammer stuck in here and when I climbed in to get it I found that I couldn't get out again.'

'Why are you building yourself in then?'

Frank was separated from Christy by a knee-high wall. She had a sudden picture of him trapped in the tiny space, bricks up to his chin and then above his head, closed into a cell of his own making.

'I thought the smoke house might work better if there wasn't this gap behind it, so while I was stuck I thought I'd get on with it. Here, give me a hand.' He climbed out, leaning heavily on Christy to keep his balance.

The gap was narrow, and in half an hour they had built their wall high and haphazard.

Frank took off his helmet and wiped his sweating forehead.

'That should do for now. We'll see if it makes a difference.'

Christy was certain it wouldn't but knew better than to say so. All around the farm there were collapsing examples of Frank's handiwork. He lined ditches with old fertiliser sacks, he mended fences with coat hangers and string and the washing machine with Superglue. None of it worked for long, but Frank was on to the next project before the binder twine unravelled on the last, and met accusations of slovenly work with bluster.

'It's broken? Nonsense, I mended it, there's nothing wrong there now.'

It was left to Christy to follow his path of construction

around the lakes with pliers, hammers and proper materials, making good his chaos.

Back in the office Frank made tea and unhelpful suggestions about Christy's price list. She often worried about what would have happened to Frank if she hadn't been there. Maybe he would have married again. She worried that her presence might be preventing this but she could not imagine him running the trout farm without her. They had learnt together and were a team now, more than Frank and Jessica had been because they shared the responsibility of the family livelihood. Christy shied from the notion that she had replaced her mother; it was a burden she knew she should not have to bear. Anyway, it was not so, for although Jessica had never known this new world, it belonged to her, built by Frank out of grief and loss and as much a monument to her as her grave.

For supper they tested the latest batch of smoked salmon, Christy hiding her reluctance by pushing pink shreds beneath her bread, and she told her father she was going to London for a few days.

'I might come too,' he joked. 'There's a match at Highbury I'd like to see.'

'We're going to stay with Aunt Vaughan.' Christy carefully sliced another slither of marble pink from the fish for Frank, her knife so sharp that the flesh came away like skin.

He passed his plate over.

'Mick won't have much fun with her,' he said. 'She gave me a real grilling when I first met her and she's only got worse with age.'

Aunt Vaughan didn't much like men or children, or for that matter most women, but she had adored Jessica, and in the absence of Jessica she had taken to adoring Christy.

She sent her silk scarves and small bottles of scent with notes scrawled in purple ink encouraging Christy to come and stay with her and be frivolous. Aunt Vaughan lived alone in a small flat where every surface was green, even the sheets. Christy always felt a little unwell staying there, but put it down to the fact that her reflection was tinted by the walls around her when she looked in the bathroom mirror.

Frank gave Christy fifty pounds as she was leaving for London with Mick. She hugged him tearfully even though she would be back on Sunday evening, and rolled the fifty-pound note up like a cigarette.

'I seem to be seeing a lot of these at the moment.' She waved the tiny baton in front of Mick's face as they drove off, and he laughed.

'You could get used to them, couldn't you, sweetheart. Mind you, don't get too expensive for me now, will you.'

Hotspur was draped like a moth-eaten rug across the back seat of the car. Christy noticed him when she turned to put her bag down and scowled.

'I didn't know you were bringing the dog. I don't think Aunt Vaughan will let him into the flat.'

'He can sleep in the car. I had to bring him because Lennie's gone back now and I haven't a soul to leave him with.'

Christy was about to ask what the point of Lennie was when she was diverted, hypnotised as she always was driving past the cemetery in Lynton. She craned her head back to try and glimpse Jessica's grave in the split-second it took to pass the gate. Mick's car radio was only just on, the windows were all closed against the spitting drizzle of late afternoon, and the upholstery wafted a mild scent of dog and aftershave. Christy was suddenly cocooned in childhood again, driving somewhere with her parents in a state of near trance, with no anxieties or responsibilities to keep her from mindlessly counting the jumping dots on the car ceiling. Jessica wore a scarf over her hair in the car and held her handbag beneath folded hands on her knee. She and Frank talked in tones the children couldn't quite hear, and although Jessica was the passenger, she stared straight ahead and never looked at Frank or into the back at the children.

Mick accelerated as they reached the motorway and Christy's reverie broke into a sweat of fear. She was remembering a winter road, darkness, a sudden blaze of headlights flooding the windscreen, Frank's voice splintering into rending tyres, the car slewing on its side in an explosion of metal and pulverised glass.

She searched wildly for something to distract Mick, hoping he would slow down if they talked.

'I'm really worried about Danny. He might have got mixed up with some unpleasant people, I think.'

The speedometer needle edged up and up; Mick glanced across at her.

'Oh yeah, why are you thinking that, sweetheart?'

The car was weaving too fast for sense between slower vehicles; it reminded Christy of the careering motion of the printer on her computer when she set it to disgorge the mailing list.

'He was showing off the other night about those bikers you took him to meet. Saying they were really marvellous, and then I found some money in his room. A fifty-pound note.'

'What did you do with it, sweetheart?'

His voice was soft beneath the roar of the engine and she could hardly hear him. She was glad because it meant she could whisper back.

'Nothing, but I was worried he might have got mixed up in drugs or something.'

Mick laughed out loud.

'Sweetheart, I don't think Danny is involved in anything. Those bikers aren't drug dealers, their lives are all about throttles and engine capacities and all that sort of thing. You wouldn't be interested and Danny was never in a moment's danger, I promise you that now, Christy.' He put his hand on her thigh. 'I gave him that money, if it's the same note, which I'm supposing it is, because he wouldn't be having more than one. It was a private joke between us which we got right into when we were working together. Don't worry about Danny, he'll soon tell you if he's hanging out with the wrong sort of people.' He seemed to consider the subject closed and returned to a low mumble of compliments for the car.

Mick had christened this new car Baby and when he drove with Danny in the front and Christy in the back she fumed with irritation as they discussed Baby and her peccadilloes. He usually restrained himself on his own with Christy, but now on the motorway he began a monologue.

'Oh Baby, you're enjoying this run. You need to let your hair down, don't you, and it's such pretty shiny hair you have, Baby, isn't it?'

'Shut up, Mick, I can't stand it. If you're going to carry on driving like this and talking to your stupid car then please let me out and I'll hitch home.' Christy was almost sobbing with terror, her feet braced against the floor, her arms nerveless rods holding her up as the car swooped in and out, on and on.

'Sweetheart, you're not jealous of Baby, are you?' Mick lounged in the driver's seat, one hand and forearm curved over the steering wheel, the other hand lolling on the gear stick, as relaxed as if he were at home watching television.

Christy bit her lip, preparing a wasp-sting retort which was eclipsed by the whine of a police siren. Behind them blue lights slewed beams into the dusk and traffic crept apologetically into the slow lane to allow the police car through.

'Jesus, man, I don't need this.' Mick braked hard and pulled over on to the hard shoulder. 'Just go along with what I say, Chris,' he whispered, and wound down his window as two policemen approached the car. 'Good afternoon there, officers,' he said. 'I'm afraid I was spending too much time looking at my beautiful girlfriend and not enough at the road.' He got out of the car.

Blushing, trembling with embarrassment, Christy stared at her feet, trying to ignore Mick and the policeman as they walked round the car. The other officer had gone back to the patrol car and was speaking on a radio, checking the car licence plates. Mick moved away towards the patrol car, and Hotspur, who had been watching, whined and started pushing his head and shoulders out of the window Mick had wound down. Christy grabbed his collar; to have the dog run over or cause an accident would be the last straw. Through the rear-view mirror she could see Mick talking while the policeman wrote notes, slanting his notebook to illuminate the page by the headlights. Mick's arms were folded, his feet planted far apart, and his hair fell across the scar on his forehead in strands. Even though he was in the wrong, his stance was confident and his presence more assured than that of the uniformed man next to him who shuffled from foot to foot and bobbed his head about in eager response to Mick's words. In the car Christy fidgeted, biting her nails and making faces at herself in the mirror. Hotspur caught her mood and whined, staring out of the back window, his head cocked to one side waiting for Mick.

The motorway was pitch dark now in the brief pauses between ribbons of white lights changing to red as cars whipped past. Christy fell into a trance of boredom and didn't know how long she had been sitting there when Mick reappeared, making her jump. He slammed the door and for once put his seat belt on then sat back and sighed.

'We got through that all right. Now let's be hitting London, sweetheart.'

I saw so many witnesses stand in the wooden box and take their oath on the Bible to tell the truth, the whole truth and nothing but the truth. At first it was odd to hear those words spoken by someone real: you associate them with films, not with life. Walking down the street in Lynton on my way to the car from court I looked at the office workers and businessmen, the builders and shoppers, the mothers on the way home with a car full of children, the students with stringy hair. I wondered how many of these ordinary people living steady lives had gone into a witness box and sworn an oath of integrity. I especially wondered about the mothers.

There was a day in court when I hated Mick. There had been days when I wished I had never met him, days when I looked across the courtroom with pity I hoped he couldn't see, and days of raw anger. But I thought I couldn't hate him, it was too late for that, and I had to help him now. I had a lot of time after his arrest to decide whether I would see him through this trial, and I vowed I would because whatever his crimes, the one thing I knew was that nobody had been hurt. Everything was confusing, and I held on to that knowledge like a shield.

I was late for the afternoon session that day; at lunchtime I had delivered three trays of trout to a new restaurant and they couldn't fit them in their fridge. In the end we put them all in the bath upstairs where the proprietor lived, banked on ice, their freckles glistening through frost chips. The witness had already been sworn in when I took my seat in the courtroom. She had neat dark hair and the side of her face I could see when she turned towards Tobin was smooth and pretty. From her skin and her voice I guessed she was about thirty-five.

Tobin was questioning her.

'So, Mrs Jackson, take your time and tell the jury in your own words what happened on the afternoon of June the 25th last year.'

Mrs Jackson cleared her throat and began.

'I picked Shelly up from playschool at about two o'clock and drove to the car-park in the centre of Melkley.'

Tobin interrupted.

'That is your local town, Mrs Jackson?'

'Yes, it's about an hour from here, sir, quite a small town.'

'Very well, carry on, Mrs Jackson.'

'Anyway, I parked and took the children to a newsagent's for some sweets. Mark was only two then and he's always a bit naughty shopping, so I bought the sweets to keep him quiet.'

Tobin again:

'Mark, your son, was in his pushchair, was he?'

Mrs Jackson nodded.

'Yes, he was in the pushchair and Shelly was holding it with me.' She paused, and when she spoke again her voice was tiny. 'I needed to go to the bank before shopping, to pay some money in for my husband.'

Tobin was gentle but insistent.

'Mrs Jackson, I know this is painful, but I don't think the jury can hear you; could you try to speak up a little?'

She threw her head back to continue. My heart thudded; I was terrified of what she was going to say.

'We went into the bank and queued for our turn. Shelly went and sat at a desk near the door because she likes drawing with the bank pens.' Mrs Jackson was crying now, but she kept going with her story, her hands kneading her handkerchief in and out of my sight. 'There was a crash suddenly, and I looked round and a man with a mask was in the bank, right next to Shelly, and he locked the door. He had a gun: I don't know if it was real or not, but I thought it was.'

'And was it from him that the crashing noise had come?'

'No, there was someone else with a mask on behind the counter with the staff. I think he had smashed a window. He had a gun as well.'

I couldn't see Mrs Jackson's face, but the jury could. The two women who liked Mick were dabbing their eyes, the man with the Roman nose had distaste arching his brows and the lines around his mouth. I looked across at Mick, but my eyes blurred tears before he saw me and I turned back to Mrs Jackson. She went on, and from the detail she supplied, I could tell she had gone over this statement a lot, and had rehearsed coming to court, determined to get it over with and say everything.

'He shouted something, the man near Shelly. I don't know what because Shelly was crying and I had to get her. I ran from the queue towards her but he had already picked her up. I thought . . .' She faltered.

Mr Sindall stood up and said, 'Your Honour, I don't think the witness need tell us what she thought.' The Judge nodded.

'Mrs Jackson, tell us what happened next.'

She gulped.

'I shouted Shelly's name and the man brought her to me. She was screaming and struggling with her arms reaching out. He gave her to me and said, "Keep your kids out of the way." I backed away to the corner where I had pushed Mark and I crouched down with the children.'

Mrs Jackson was trembling. I could see fear through her tidy courtroom clothes; she leant forwards on the witness box. If I had been Tobin I would have finished there. There cannot have been a soul in court unaffected by Mrs Jackson's evidence.

But before anyone could gather their thoughts Tobin was probing.

'Mrs Jackson, may I just stop you for a moment? Could you describe either of the men, their clothing, their accents, anything about them?'

She shook her head.

'The thing I noticed was the gun. Both of them had guns.'

'Can you describe the guns, please, Mrs Jackson.'

'I'm sorry, I can't. I have tried to remember more; it was all so fast and yet so slow, I can only remember the children screaming. I had to look after them.'

I couldn't listen any longer, I couldn't go through with this woman's ordeal. I pushed my way past the two men on the end of my row in the public gallery and out of the courtroom. It would look bad for Mick that I left like this, but I didn't care. Why should I? He hadn't cared about Mrs Jackson and her children in the Melkley bank last summer.

I didn't go and see him after court that day; I drove home instead and went down to the lake. During the trial it was easy to forget there was a real world dazzling in late spring. I sat on the grass and afternoon sun warmed me to the bone. I watched a family of ducklings scull across the lake, their small feet invisible oars beneath the surface. Trees shimmering in the breeze and a distant mower were all I could hear. It was so peaceful by the lake. I wished I did not have to go back to the court; I wanted to go into the house this afternoon and get on with my life on the trout farm without ever having to think about Mick again. I could do it, he couldn't stop me, he was locked up. And he trusted me.

I remembered a visit we'd had before Christmas when he was still on remand. He was smiling and confident; he said he had a present for me. It had to go and be checked by security, but at the end of the visit he was allowed to give it to me. I shut my eyes and the guards brought it round the screen and placed it in my hands. A small pink bear made of felt. It burnt my hands as if it were made of ice.

'I made it,' he whispered, leaning forwards so our conversation could be private. 'They've got a soft-toy class here, it's packed out, all the cons love it, but I swapped with someone and got one session so I could make this for you. Keep it on your bed, sweetheart, to remind you of me.'

The pink bear came home and I put it at the bottom of my bed. I hated it. It glowed with love and it made me cry. I couldn't bear to think of Mick sewing pink felt ears and paws.

9

Jessica went to the doctor out of spite. She hoped there was something wrong with her, something to make Frank and Charlie feel guilty. A web of exhaustion smothered her, her eyelids drooped when she was driving, when she was cooking, when she was trying to have a conversation with one of her children through a closed bedroom door. They rarely stayed in a room with her long enough for her to speak, so she had taken to pursuing them around the house until they slammed into their bedrooms. Everything was unsatisfactory and everything was filthy.

Mrs Edge, the cleaning lady, had decided to move to southern Spain, and now only came to the house to sit with a cup of coffee and regale Jessica with her plans.

'Ernie's been out there now for a month and he's found a very nice new house just behind the car-park. Of course I asked whether there was a garden for the dogs, but Ernie, bless him, he was so excited about the golf, he hadn't looked. We'll have a front drive and we might plant some of those evergreen trees. I think they grow in Spain – we don't want those Spanish-style cactuses or anything.' On she went, unheeding of Jessica's set smile or of the sink full of washing up.

Dust banked beneath beds and sofas and the ironing pile bulged, spewing shirts and pillowcases out of the airing cupboard and across the bathroom where Danny trod mud from his football boots over them. Jessica tried to clear up, but by the time she had done the kitchen after breakfast each morning black spots danced behind her eyes and singing dizziness forced her to sit down and rest. She had stopped going to work for Charlie, and had decided to tell him it was over. But when she saw him her resolve vanished. He was so concerned, so charming and so interested in her. Next time would do.

She planned to have lunch with him after her doctor's appointment, to announce her illness, which she imagined would be diagnosed as something Victorian and romantic like a decline.

But Dr Fellowes was inconclusive.

'I will make an appointment for you at the hospital. We must do some blood tests, Mrs Naylor.'

A chill descended in his consulting room. Jessica rose.

'I've got cancer, haven't I?' Dr Fellowes had a prominent jaw muscle – she saw it quiver as he swallowed.

'That is not a conclusion we jump to. Blood tests are routine in a case such as yours. There is no evidence of cancer as yet.'

Jessica nodded, not even trying to believe him.

'So I will hear from the hospital, will I?' She pulled her coat tight around her to hide her trembling limbs.

Dr Fellowes swallowed again; the jaw had a spasm.

'Yes, don't worry, I must stress that it's purely routine at this stage.'

Jessica left the surgery and walked out into Lynton. A bus roared by flecking damp dust over her feet as she waited on the pavement. She looked at its wheels, black and dripping from a puddle. It would be so easy.

She told no one about her visit to the doctor or her

subsequent trip to the hospital for blood tests. She was biding her time. The results came through, but she hadn't needed them. The consultant's solicitousness was touching but unnecessary. She told Frank and the children on Hallowe'en. Someone else told Charlie.

The family were sitting at the table after supper when Jessica said, 'I am dying of cancer.' No preamble, just five words.

Christy couldn't see anyone's face or clothes, just the shapes of them silhouetted in a room fragmenting like a shattered windscreen. She remembered the car crash long ago. The sensations were the same, everything imploding, sinking inward to a black dot. In the car crash the radio had carried on playing, and the words of that song came back to her now:

> If you've got leaving on your mind,
> Hurt me now, get it over,
> Tell me now, get it over,
> If there's a new love in your heart.

They had all been expecting her to say she was going. Leaving with Charlie to lead a life full of satinwood furniture and sin. Christy hadn't been to church since childhood, but she believed her mother was committing a sin and she hated her for it. Now it was different. She wasn't going with Charlie after all.

Aunt Vaughan, clad in a pink satin négligé, mules and diaphanous nightdress, swooped on Christy, chattering, black eyes darting over Mick as she kissed her god-daughter.
'You're so late, I couldn't think what had happened to you.

I've saved some mussels, so delicious, and I know you never have them at home. Come in, come in and have a drink.'

She shook hands with Mick, her sagging face tightening into flirtation as instinctively as the schooling of features before a looking-glass; chin down, kohl-rimmed eyes widened, a half smile lifting the red droop of her lips.

'Well, Christy, he's very handsome,' she murmured, as Mick disappeared to the spare bedroom to deposit the bags. 'He reminds me of someone, I can't think who, but it will come to me. Jessica would have loved him.'

She and Christy moved through to the sitting room where Spanish music tinkled from behind a screen. They sat down facing one another by the gas-coal fire. Vaughan's pink mules sank into the depths of the carpet, and her dressing gown hissed as it met the drum-tight stuffing of the armchair. Christy lit a cigarette and tucked her feet up under her, twisting to look around the room, already feeling faintly sick as she absorbed the viridian energy of the walls. Layer upon layer of colour built up from pale silver in the hall through the kitchen bright as newly podded peas and on into the splendour of the sitting room where everything not green was gold except for Vaughan herself.

She lay back in her chair like a prawn on a bed of lettuce and gave a little cry.

'I knew I'd remember. Christy, have you noticed what you've done? Mick looks just like Charlie. Remember Charlie? Your father was so upset, of course, and Jessica paid no attention. I must say, charming as Charlie was, I did see Frank's point, and of course it never really was resolved, was it?' On she went, crossing and uncrossing her white ankles, waving her hands to amplify a story Christy never liked hearing, unravelling the lace of protection Mick and her happiness with him had woven since last seeing Vaughan.

Mick came into the room and Vaughan's voice flew with amusement.

'Yes, yes, you even frown like Charlie. Dear me, how history repeats itself. Of course he didn't have a scar but otherwise the likeness is startling.'

Christy didn't move; she closed her eyes, saw green and opened them again. Mick stroked her hair, silenced himself by Vaughan's sing-song monologue. Christy couldn't look at him. All her excitement at coming to London had vanished. Vaughan had spoilt it through tactless, pointless gabble; Mick had spoilt it through being stopped by the police. They were taking away her pleasure, her unique love affair, tarnishing every aspect so none of it was hers and none of it was safe.

Vaughan tripped off to the kitchen to bring in the mussels and Mick knelt in front of Christy, leaning close to whisper, 'Shall we go? I've got a few mates we could stay with, you know.'

All the nausea and anger rolling through Christy slowed and collapsed into exhaustion and she shook her head.

'No, it's fine here; she'll calm down. Please don't pay any attention to her, she's drunk. She's imagining things.'

'So what are you doing in London, Mick? Are you here to make money or spend it?' Vaughan staggered back in under a heaped tray, bearing most of the weight on the jut of her bosom.

Mick took the tray and it shrank as it passed from Vaughan's diminutive clutch into his hands.

'I'm here to spend money on Christy. We'll be going to the shops tomorrow and finding whatever she wants.'

Vaughan clutched his arm as he put the tray down on a small table.

'Goodness, I meant to ask you, did you see anything of the robbery this morning?'

'What robbery? Where?' asked Christy.

'In Lynton, of course. Can you believe it? It was on the news.' Vaughan shuddered and announced, 'They had guns.' She continued, 'There was a raid on the main bank this morning. They said there have been a few violent robberies in the area. You've probably read about them.' She gulped more gin, swilling it in her mouth and swallowing loudly.

Mick brought a bowl of mussels over to Christy, bruise-blue shells half open like castanets clacking in time to Aunt Vaughan's music. Vaughan shuffled behind the screen and turned the volume up, then singing along, she danced a few steps in front of Christy's chair. Mick leant against the mantelpiece, his arm stretched along Vaughan's candlesticks and photographs, one foot propped on the fender, looming among her fragile colours and small treasures. His face was expressionless: only his eyes moved, following Vaughan as she tripped and skipped across the carpet.

'I do hate violence, don't you?' Vaughan shimmied up to the fireplace, her head hanging back, eyes rolling up to Mick as she danced on. 'I've nothing against people robbing banks – after all, the insurance company pays – but to use guns is another matter.'

Christy started laughing, Mick covered his face with his hands but his shoulders shook with mirth. Vaughan billowed on, her dressing gown raked back and resting across her elbows, her hands on her hips to accentuate the snakish steps she used to cross and recross the room.

'She's drunk that whole bottle of gin this evening,' Christy whispered to Mick. 'She has one every day. It's amazing she isn't dead.' Vaughan spluttered into song again, Christy tugged at Mick's arm, pulling him down next to her. 'She's pretty loopy after about six in the evening; all that stuff about you looking like Charlie is just mad.'

Charlie had come to Jessica's funeral. Christy saw him outside the circle of mourners, standing alone with his hands in the pockets of his long grey coat, all his muscles hunched, curving him forwards from his spine like a totem pole topped by his still shaggy hair. The hair was grey too, but maybe it always had been. She hadn't seen him since Jessica announced her illness six months before, but it did not surprise her that he had come; Jessica would have wanted him there. She wanted anyone who had loved her to be there. It didn't matter to her that Charlie's presence might upset others: it was her funeral, her last chance for ever, and other people's feelings were second to her own. She didn't quite invite people, but in the weeks leading up to her death she told her visitors that they must be there 'to make it a perfect day, a fond farewell, not a cold-hearted one'. This made the visitors cry, but Jessica was halfway to another world now, and so deeply barbed by her own pain that she could no longer be touched by anyone else's.

Christy didn't speak to Charlie at the funeral. She would have done, but when she searched the sober-faced crowd he was gone and Jessica's friends had formed a well-mannered queue as if at a wedding, offering damp kisses and condolences to the family.

Vaughan was talking to Mick now, telling him about Jessica's bravery, her dignity, her marvellous funeral. Christy closed her eyes and thought about Charlie. She wasn't angry with him now, or with her mother for loving him. Jessica had paid with her life, Charlie with his loss. Now she had Mick, and she knew about love too.

*   *   *

146

The thud and judder of traffic woke Christy early and she lay still as grey light slid in between the net curtains of Aunt Vaughan's spare room. In the adjacent twin bed Mick slept on, the black stubble on his chin framed by frilled pillows, making him look like the wolf in 'Little Red Riding Hood'. Christy got up and dressed, tiptoeing around the small room so as not to wake him, and crept into the hall. Vaughan's bedroom door was open and from the warm darkness wafted the smell of stale scent and alcohol. Christy paused outside but heard nothing.

A slime of squalor lay across the kitchen. Onion peelings curved like toy boats bobbed on the cooker beside a tower of saucepans and bowls. Water cobbled with mussel shells half filled the sink and Christy prodded at the plughole through a swirl of tea leaves as she filled the kettle. She opened the window and noise and air flooded in, drowning the depressing glug of drains unblocking and diluting the brackish smell of old fish. Christy's tea tasted of brine. She spat it back into the cup and began clearing up. Vaughan, with the sixth sense of the slovenly, came into the kitchen as the last plate and spoon were dried and stacked on the table.

'Good morning, my love. What an angel you are to have cleared up; thank you.' She opened a carton of grapefruit juice and grimacing horribly drank from it at length. 'This stuff is so ghastly, but one must have vitamin C.'

Christy leant against the sink, her face in shadows, her hair streaming light from the window behind her. The Vaughan before her now had so little to do with the Vaughan whose commands and ice-hard discipline had frightened her as a child. Drink had softened her, gnawing away at her hard heart as rot eats an apple until she was left soft and puffy when touched, sweetly rancid and sad in a way

147

that was more frightening than her sternest demeanour had ever been.

She squinted at Christy, wiping grapefruit juice away from her lips with the back of her hand.

'You look more and more like your mother: dear me, how sad. I must say, I walked in on Mick in the bathroom. Most attractive in a brutish way, isn't he?'

Christy sighed.

'You said that last night, Aunt Vaughan, remember? When you said he reminded you of Charlie.'

'Did I? Heavens, it's so easy to forget things these days. But what does he do? He looks like a gangster with that huge coat. Of course, he wasn't wearing it in the bathroom, but he still looked as though he was. You know what I mean, don't you?'

Christy was spared the trouble of answering by Mick's appearance in the kitchen. He had his coat on.

'Good morning, Vaughan,' he said, looking at Christy. 'I think we should be going out now, sweetheart. Are you ready?'

Vaughan ushered them into the hall, jangling sets of keys and babbling.

'Where are you going? Shall I meet you for lunch? What time will you be back? Here, these are the keys; you use this one for the front door and this little bent one to get into the building.'

They closed the front door behind themselves and Mick whistled.

'Phew, I never thought I'd be getting you out of there, not till she was unconscious again anyway.'

Christy laughed, carefree now Vaughan was safely out of sight, holding hands with Mick as they walked down the street to the car. She wanted to take the tube or the bus.

'Come on, we're in London, we'll be stuck in traffic jams with the car,' but Mick shook his head.

'We'll need it for your shopping, you know, and I don't like to leave it here, it might be towed away or nicked or something.'

From Vaughan's flat in Islington it was less than a page on the A to Z to reach Camden Market where Maisie had assured Christy she would find everything she could ever want. Christy steered Mick faultlessly through the one-way system and to a car-park in the derelict husk of an old building.

He was impressed.

'Not many people are any good at map reading. I could get you a job with that skill.'

She moved closer to him, protected from the streaming jostle by his arm across her shoulders. Christy hadn't been to London without Maisie before; she hadn't ever felt like coming on her own, it was too great a step to take. Wandering through the market with Mick, lingering at a stall to run her fingers through a rack of stiff clothes or a table strewn with hats made of pink velvet, she felt serene and happy. This was what people with boyfriends did. There they were, all around her, couples holding hands, walking in step with one another, laughing over an extravagant pair of ballooning trousers or screening one another from the gusting wind while two cigarettes were lit.

She could smell the boot stall before she saw it. New leather gleamed dark in a corner of the market where racks of boots formed a three-sided room covered by swagged awning and carpeted erratically with stepping stones made of flattened cardboard boxes. No one was there, not even the stall holder. Just boots shackled to the stands. Christy sat down on one of the low stools and took off her shoes.

A short round man scuttled into the stall, stuffing the last billow of a doughnut into his mouth.

'What can I do for you?' He winked at Christy and his eye vanished into a fold of flesh itself almost obscured by the greasy mop of ringlets growing from one point on top of his head.

Christy told him her size and he unlocked half a rack of boots, his hands a whirl among the chains.

'Try what you like, miss.' He turned as Mick came in and gave a small cry.

'I remember you, fella. You was trying on boots for hours in here, wasn't ya? You bought a good pair too, if I remember.' He peered down at Mick's feet. 'Not wearing them now, though, are ya?'

Mick stepped back, slipping on a wet wedge of cardboard.

'Woops, mind yer don't fall there, fella.' The little stall holder put out a hand to steady Mick.

'I haven't been here before.' Mick's voice was almost a whisper. Christy glanced up from trying on, startled by the odd way he was talking. 'You must have got me confused with someone else.'

Grizzled curls spun as the man shook his head.

'Na, na, mate. It was you. I remember that mean old scar of yours.' His money pouch bounced with his belly as he laughed. 'It wasn't so long ago. You must be a busy fella to have forgotten.'

'What do you think of these, Mick?' Christy waved a foot sheathed in black biker's leather and jingling with zips.

He scowled.

'You don't want that sort, do you, sweetheart? I was thinking we'd be buying something a bit pretty.'

The stall holder watched both of them, jocularity forgotten as he saw a sale ebb away. He picked Christy's foot up, hands cupped beneath her heel as if he were raising a trophy to be photographed.

'They look dead smart,' he pronounced.

'I thought I was allowed to choose.' Christy bristled with embarrassment, pulling her foot away from the man's hands.

Mick sighed.

'How much are they?'

'Well.' The man had his head on one side, observing the boots with doting fondness. He pursed his lips then nodded. 'Yes, I'll do it. To you, two hundred and fifty quid, cash, of course.'

Christy bit her lip and started unzipping the boots. She hadn't realised how expensive they would be and she trembled with irritation at her own stupidity.

'Put them back on, I'm not carrying them.' Mick handed the beaming stall holder a stack of notes still bound by the white bank wrapper. 'Something tells me you aren't going to be beaten down.'

Both Christy and the fat man thought he was addressing them and they answered in unison. 'Oh Mick, you mustn't. I never thought they'd cost – '

'You know that from last time, don't ya, fella? You'll be able to wear 'em together now. I like a unisexual boot.'

Mick pulled Christy away and out of the stall and marched her off through the market, his face clouded and angry. This was not how Christy had imagined their day's shopping. Trotting to keep up, her old shoes banging against her side, the new boots squeaking and jingling, she pulled at his sleeve.

'What's wrong, Mick?'

'That bloke wound me up. I'm sorry.' Mick forced a smile and hugged her.

Christy squeezed his hand and whispered, 'Thank you for the boots.'

Vaughan was crestfallen when they came back to change.

'I thought we'd have a lovely evening together. Do you really want to go to a party in some dreadful dive?' She had Christy at bay in the kitchen, her face too close, her eyes unblinking pits of loneliness.

'Mick's already said we'll go. I'm sorry, Aunt Vaughan. This is the first time we've been away together and Mick planned it all. But you'll have Hotspur.' The dog wagged his tail.

He was enjoying London. Vaughan let him sleep on her bed. She turned to stroke him and Christy sidled past and into the spare bedroom where Mick was stretched out on one of the beds with his coat on. He hadn't even taken off his shoes and he was pretending to be asleep. Christy had floated on a stream of pleasure all day. Mick shed his odd behaviour as soon as he had paid for her boots. A dress followed lunch in a café and Mick telling her she was beautiful.

In the afternoon they had separated for a while. Mick said he had to see someone in a bar. She took the underground into the West End and found the perfect birthday present for him. It lay in a dark-green box carefully hidden among her new clothes. Christy didn't know what had made her go into the shop; the entrance was guarded by a liveried doorman and inside glass cabinets displayed tiny items sunk into heavy velvet. The pen was in a side cabinet presided over by a pale youth, without eyebrows or lashes. He took it out for her, rolling it over and over in his hand as he explained its virtues. She wasn't listening, she gazed at the silver streak on his palm and knew she would buy it, no matter how much it cost. Mick would keep it in his top pocket and wherever he went it would be with him, a memento of her, a solid silver wand to charm the thoughts out of his head.

Without thinking she wrote 'I love you' on the sheet of cream paper the youth had given her to test it on. His forehead blotched scarlet and he coughed. Christy snatched the paper away, crumpling it, suddenly noticing the expensive quiet of the shop in which the twisting of a piece of paper cracked like a gun going off. Back at the flat she dragged all her bags into the bathroom and sat on the floor delving among soft folds for the box. The pen had cost almost as much as her boots. Her heart raced at the thought of such extravagance. Her savings had been bitten in half but it didn't matter, it was a perfect present.

The party was held in an old warehouse beyond any part of London Christy had ever been to before. She shivered in her thin dress waiting for Mick to lock the car, daunted by the vast darkness of the walls, the broken windows on the lower floors like punched-out eyes dangling shards of glass. On the top floor lights swung out in beams of pink and blue and yellow and the music was so loud Christy could feel it as much as hear it. They walked up a zigzag metal staircase on the outside of the building, Christy clutching Mick's coat from behind, too terrified to look out and see East London twinkling around her. For a craven moment she wished she was at home with Frank, cooking supper to eat in front of the television while she told him about her time in London.

The moment Mick walked in a man with a beard called out to him and he was swallowed by the relentless beat of the party. He moved away from Christy to talk and she lost him in the heaving shoal of people. Faces with unseeing eyes swam past her where she paused, ghostly in her grey dress, her hair a transparent shawl over her shoulders. No one seemed to be talking. In aimless drifts they crossed and recrossed the room, grouping for a moment at the bar then moving off to darker corners. On the dance floor a woman wrapped in red silk spun and twirled in front of two swaying men who stared over her head at nothing. Christy wondered which of the glass faces belonged to the host and hostess. Mick had said they were old friends and she had expected a recognisable uniform of jeans and dark jackets, floral dresses and cheap jewellery. Instead there were boiler suits and sweeps of floating silk, strong colour dappled like oil on water, and she searched in vain for a familiar expression, a set of features she could recognise.

Mick touched her shoulder, and she turned.

'This is Linda. She says you've met.'

Pointed teeth laced a smile in Linda's small mouth.

'Hello, Christy. We met at that hen party, do you remember?'

'You should have a massage from Linda some time, sweetheart; she can work wonders, let me tell you.'

Why was Linda here? Out of place, wrong in her faded black skirt and tasselled Indian shirt, all that hennaed hair piled up and wispy. Mick must have told her to come. She didn't belong any more than Christy did.

Christy draped her arms around Mick, smiling at Linda.

'Nice to see you. Are you enjoying the party?'

Linda licked her lips, looking at Mick as she answered, not at Christy.

'Well, I don't know anyone, but Mick introduced me to a few of his friends, so it's not too bad.'

A blade of jealousy slid into Christy.

'Let's go, Mick, I want to go home.'

'We've only been here for a minute, now come on, Chris, let your hair down.' Mick reached across to Linda as he spoke and pulled the comb from her heaped hair.

Christy's nails flexed on his shirt and she stopped herself digging them in by clenching her fists.

'I'm going to dance.' She spoke in a brittle shiny voice; a matching smile stretched across her face.

Mick followed her and they moved over to the dance floor where the loudspeakers hummed and there was no possibility of conversation. Christy loved dancing. When she stepped on to the platform with the other dancers they fell back around her and watched. She didn't notice, she just danced. Hammering, pulsing music, one rhythm over and over, forcing thought away into a white throb somewhere, nowhere. No thought, just limbs flying loosened and feet burning, unable to stop. A skin of sweat under clothes, hot and tight, not bursting into drops, stretching hotter and tighter, thirst swelling inside until nothing remained of the flesh.

Coming off the dance floor half an hour later, Christy shivered, her dress wrinkled and damp as if she had wrung it out and put it on. Her face shone beneath streaked hair and she moved to the bar and drank from a bottle of water in one determined movement. It could wait no longer. She had to talk to Mick; she was strong now and it was time to fill in the holes she had turned away from. Weightless, fearless expectation sharpened her senses.

She picked Mick's coat up from a chair by the door.

'We're going,' she said.

His eyes were too dark to see, but he didn't go and say goodbye to Linda hovering nearby. He threw his coat over

Christy's shoulders, swathing her so only her head and her hair were lit, gliding down the fire escape and into the jet-stamped night.

Afterwards Christy looked back on that episode and saw brief scenes pared down and sharp as glass. They had sat in the car somewhere on the edge of the Thames facing thick flowing water, side by side in wells of silence bridged by Christy's questions and Mick's slow answers. He said he bought and sold cars because his journalism made so little money. He was good at fixing cars, he said; that was why he always had cash. He had not published much work, not as much as he had led her to believe. He said he loved her and she was his only chance.

Warm in his coat, Christy prodded each confession, tidying every loose end, securing it before she would let it go and move on to the next. She radiated crisp confidence, the end of her cigarette flaring red around her, a barrier protecting her from the heap of Mick slumped in shadow behind the steering wheel. He said he had invited Linda to the party. She was a good friend to him and he owed her a favour.

'What favour?' Christy snorted a plume of smoke from her nostrils, smudging yellow edges on to clouded darkness.

'Oh, she stood by me in some trouble long ago.'

'What trouble?' Hauling slowly, she hooked out of him a sordid memory of embezzling a social-security cheque.

Her feelings about Mick were altered irrevocably that night. She could not trust him again, and he could no longer make her safe. But he had given her so much by loving her. After he had told her the whole story, she heard a voice inside her: You don't need him any more. He has given you the confidence to walk away.

*   *   *

156

To change the sinking mood they drove for a while and crossed the river, joining a chain of lorries slowing and stopping at a series of floodlit warehouses. The fish market. They walked through the halls, their feet slapping echo into the roof as the traders arrived. Christy was diverted, marching ahead, breathing deep the salt-wet air, leaning over great plastic trays ice-studded and sliding with fish. Under glaring neon men bustled trolleys stacked high and dripping across the concrete expanse. Each trolley bore a tower of heaving crates from which tails and fins jutted, trembling and wet. Mick followed her hunched in his coat, stopping where she did, grunting when forced to respond. A crate of blue lobsters, their claws clamped shut with orange tape, overbalanced at Mick's feet. He jumped away, looking at Christy to see what to do.

'Oh, poor things.' She was on her knees immediately, straightening the crate, gently reaching for the lobsters. Claws waved close to her face, long antennae twisting black against her skin as she picked them up and re-housed them in the crate. 'Help me, Mick, they're escaping.' Scuttling on hobbled limbs, two of the lobsters headed off beneath a table.

Christy looked round for Mick: he shook his head.

'I can't touch them, Chris, I'm sorry.'

Forgetting her dress she crawled after them.

A lorry driver whistled, 'Lovely legs, darling,' as she emerged pink-cheeked, a crustacean in each hand.

Mick took a deep breath and tried a joke.

'They'll be the same colour as your face when they're cooked, sweetheart.'

She looked at him and smiled.

'Let's go.'

*   *   *

Dawn was breaking when they returned to Vaughan's flat. As the sun breathed colour into the sky, the faces of buildings they passed grew stronger, neat rows of front doors drawing light back into paintwork turned monochrome in the night-lit streets.

Mick parked and turned to Christy.

'Are you tired?'

She shook her head. It was six o'clock on an October Saturday morning and she thought she would never need sleep again.

'I reckon we could be in Lynton for breakfast.' Mick glanced at her, checking her response before she answered. He was hesitant and uncertain, daunted by Christy's radiant confidence.

'I'd like that,' she said. There was no point in being in London with him now. She needed time to think.

On tiptoe they entered the flat and without speaking tidied the bedroom. Hotspur yawned when Mick called him and had to be carried to the car. Christy attached a note for Vaughan to the fridge, tucking it under a scrawled memo Vaughan had written to herself in violent black strokes, forgetting punctuation. 'VODKA SHOT GLASSES GAS MAN'. Christy thought it would make a good headline for a tabloid. In the sleeping street they heaped their bags into the car on top of the dozing dog. Christy opened her door to get in.

Mick pulled her back, hugging her, whispering, 'I need you, sweetheart, I need you.'

She did not answer.

Danny gave evidence, so did Dad, but not me. They said my evidence was not worth having because I was not an impartial witness. I didn't want Mick to ask Dad to give evidence. It was wrong to embroil him in this mess.

But Dad surprised me.

'Mick needs support. I will happily stand up in court and tell the jury what I know of his character. Where's the harm in it?' We didn't discuss whether or not Mick was guilty, not even right after the arrest. 'It's not for us to pass judgement,' Dad insisted.

Danny was a strange sight in a suit. An Adam's apple jutted above the knot of his tie and his neck was like a flower stem, long and thin, bound by his shirt collar. The suit was grey, a few shades darker than his face before he went into the courtroom. He knew about the armed guards because I had told him, but he flinched when they searched him, sticking his arms out straight as a scarecrow's in the big folds of grey flannel. He had cut his hair for his court appearance and slicked it back with water, emphasising the small neatness of his head. Facing the jury across the yellow-lit courtroom the innocence of youth shone all over Danny; Tobin with his jowls, his five o'clock shadow and his red-veined nose was as coarse as a pantomime dame in contrast. Everyone knew Danny was my brother, and the public gallery was packed with ghouls who had come to see how entwined the Naylors were with the case. Even though the press could not release Mick's name and we hadn't talked about it to anyone, the whole of Lynton seemed to know.

Danny had to talk about the time he found the parking ticket on Mick's car. It was as if he were walking blindfolded along a cliff. Tobin pushed him, encouraging him towards the edge, trying to make him say something which would swoop him into betraying Mick.

'You gave a statement to the police in which you stated that you found a parking ticket on Mr Fleet's car dated June the 25th. Can you tell the jury about this incident, Mr Naylor?'

I shook my hair over my face so no one would see my shock. This was the date of Mrs Jackson's ordeal in the bank. A giant jigsaw was nearing completion and none of us had known we were working on it. Danny didn't know about Mrs Jackson, he hadn't been in court.

He was filling in the pieces for Tobin who rocked on his heels with triumph flickering across his lips.

'I found the parking ticket on the car at about nine o'clock,' said Danny. 'I gave it to Mick – to Mr Fleet, I mean, and he put it in his pocket.'

'Mr Naylor, what is it about this incident that made it stay in your mind for nearly a year?'

Danny hesitated before answering, and his voice was sharp with surprise.

'Well, the police asked me about it when I gave my statement. I don't know if it would have stayed in my mind otherwise.'

Tobin glowered: Danny was proving an irritating witness. He was clearly telling the truth, and his answers were calm and bland. The jury liked the look of Danny; even the old lady whose fingers twitched for her knitting had creases of benevolence around her mouth. By now I knew enough about court not to be surprised that Tobin was gentle with Danny. The barristers were always nice to the witnesses the jury favoured; they didn't want to risk becoming disliked.

The cross examination from Mr Sindall was brief and by lunchtime Danny had finished. It was so unsensational I was almost disappointed. As we filed out of court for the lunch break I realised I had not looked across at Mick all morning.

160

Dad didn't give evidence until later in the trial. He was a character witness for Mick along with Linda. Dad hadn't been to the prison so hadn't seen Mick for months. They smiled at one another before Dad took his oath and tears stung my eyes when I saw them. I had let Dad down by meeting Mick and falling in love. It was wrong of me to have been party to their friendship because now Dad was paying the price in the witness box. I had cheated on his dignity. I should never have let it go this far. His responses to the questions put to him rang out louder and louder until he was one decibel below shouting. I smiled, guessing what was going through his head: The louder I am the more truthful I am. He believed it and so, by the look of them, did the jury, all twelve alert and cheerful for once.

'Mick Fleet was and still is my daughter's boyfriend. I have known him for a little more than a year and I have found him reliable and honest to deal with. I know nothing of the events that have caused this case to be brought and can say without reservation that Mick Fleet as I know him is an honourable man.' Dad paused. I was sure he was going to cry.

My skin tingled pink and electric. I thought this must be how people feel on their wedding day, when the person they love is represented in a glow of good cheer; I began to giggle insanely. Danny nudged me, but I couldn't stop. He pulled me to my feet and out of the courtroom before Dad had finished. Outside I spluttered laughter and tried to light a cigarette. Everyone lit cigarettes the second they came out of court into the waiting area; it was as natural to me now as shutting my eyes to sneeze.

'I'm sorry, Danny, I'm really sorry. I just had the most ridiculous thoughts in there. I think the strain of all this is getting to me now.'

Maisie appeared from the main stairs. She had lost

interest in the case, having yawned her way through three days in court, and only came now to check when it was going to end.

She marched up to us glaring.

'Has Dad finished yet? They must have got enough by now.'

The date of her wedding loomed two weeks away and she was afraid the case might still be going on. Dad still hoped she might change her mind and pretended it wasn't happening.

'Have you sent Mick an invitation?' Danny couldn't help teasing her, and she swallowed any bait he cast.

'Of course I bloody haven't. He's in prison.'

'He might be out by then. He might be found innocent.'

'He's guilty as hell. He'll get twenty years.' Her mouth stretched back in a snarl.

I pushed her.

'Shut up, Maisie, everyone can hear you.'

The guards outside the courtroom were motionless with their guns, but I knew they were listening. Maisie dragged me away to the top of the stairs.

'Look, you've got to find out how much longer this is all going to take. I need to know.'

'You're not the only one, Maisie.' Her selfishness was reassuring, a thread of consistency running through bolts of woven confusion.

'Look, Christy, I know this is difficult for you, but a joke is a joke. You can't stand by him. He's dangerous and he *has* lied to you. Even if he does get off, how can you trust him? He might be checking Dad's house out to raid.'

Her mouth gaped and closed, gaped and closed as she harangued me. I was half listening, but my concentration on her words dwindled to nothing. She was being Mum,

162

I realised. Talking sense or talking self. Whichever it was, she was saying what my mother would have said. I wished I could tell her that I knew she was right.

A door beside us opened and Mick's barrister emerged. I smiled and he moved nearer to me.

'Could I have a word with you, Christy?'

Maisie snorted and swung away muttering, 'This whole thing is like a bad television programme and bloody Christy thinks she's the star.'

Mr Sindall's eyebrows curled in astonishment but otherwise he pretended not to hear.

'Your father was very good. A solid character witness speaks volumes to a jury.'

I twisted one leg round the other and nodded. Whenever Sindall spoke to me I felt as though I was in the headmistress's office at school. His lips were red and curved around square yellow teeth, and out of the courtroom in his gown with the greasy periwig perched on top of greying hair, he was difficult to take seriously. In court he was fine. I loved watching him pull the veins of Tobin's arguments until they snapped and clotted to dry uselessness in the minds of the jurors. He never needed to blink and his still approach was very different from Tobin's bluster. He was sinister where Tobin was bullying, he was a shark where Tobin was a bullfrog.

'We're nearly there now, Christy. Mick is not giving evidence, as you know, and tomorrow Mr Tobin and I will present our speeches, the Judge will sum up on Wednesday and by the end of the week we should have a verdict.'

'Oh good,' I said, and wondered if it was.

The surface of the feeding pen boiled, hungry mouths gaping, sinking, tails spilling circles in pursuit of a pellet of food beneath cross-hatched netting. The jetty planks trembled under Christy's feet, reverberations setting the next pen swarming. She moved on, buckets thumping her calves, bruising through her trousers on to a patch of skin always tender when she was on a week of feeding duty. The third pen was still. Christy flung a handful of feed in and waited. No fish rose to snap the surface tension; the water gleamed black, frilled white with the reflection of passing cloud. At one corner of the pen something bobbed beneath the waterline then another form and another. She peered across, leaning to see into the corner, trying to make sense of the clogged shapes emerging, her heart drumming apprehension. The fish were dead. She knew this before she saw maimed carcasses drift to the netting at the edge, broken as if vast hands had picked them up and torn through scales and skin, flesh and gossamer bone.

Christy had reared these fish from tiny fry, watched them grow with as much affection as anyone could have for creatures never seen but for the churn of mouths and tails until they were hooked on a fisherman's line. Now they were dead, floating in blood-boultered water. She paced along the jetty, fists clenched, searching for explanations in the fenced square of lake. Then she saw the heron. Dead too. Caught in the netting of the pen, mud-coated where its wings had tried to beat freedom. On its beak just beneath the water, skewered and shivering spectral energy, hung a once perfect rainbow trout. Christy leaned over the edge of the jetty, stretching out her arms, but was too far away to reach the bird. Pulling herself back she caught sight of a second heron enmeshed beneath her. This one was alive, blue-silver feathers floating like little tug boats around its bulk, torn

164

out in the struggle to escape the netting web. Beneath a curve brow its eye was a disc of watchful unblinking yellow awaiting death or deliverance.

Christy ran back to the house shouting for Frank. Maisie met her in the hall. It was her day off and she had come early to talk to Frank about dates next year for her wedding. As Christy had feared, Anna's nuptials had affected her. Worn down by her bullying letters, Ben had finally agreed that spring would be appropriate, particularly apple-blossom time which Maisie felt suited her well.

Frank was out. Maisie lurched on high snakeskin heels across to the lake with Christy. Armed with nets and sticks, Christy ran ahead, her unfastened waders quacking and flapping around her legs.

'Oh God, how disgusting.' Maisie covered her face with her hands, shuddering as Christy took off her coat and opened the nets over the surface of the pen to lower herself into the water.

The waders were not a good idea. Bubbles oozed around her and water spilled over in a trickle then a torrent.

'It's much deeper than I thought.' Christy heaved herself out again leaving the boots crumpling beneath the weight of water and took off her jeans. 'Here, you get those boots out and I'll get the heron.'

She slid down, suppressing panic as her feet sank deep into cold velvet mud. Backed against netting at eye-level, the heron was nearer and bigger than Christy anticipated. Its beak was an arrow pointing at her face; she could see in her mind the dead bird at the other side of the pen and its impaled prey; she imagined her eyeball pierced, or her arm as she reached to free the bird.

'Catch it in this.' Maisie crouched on the jetty waving Christy's coat. 'Otherwise it'll stab you.'

Christy caught the coat, the heron opened its beak in a silent snarl, two compass points pivoting inches away, between them a tongue curled in disdain. She lurched forwards trailing the coat into the water and threw it over the heron; heavy fabric bore the hidden head of the bird down, wet staining the coat creeping black across sandy oilskin. The heron struggled and its beak began to protrude; the coat was slipping off as the bird fought its way free. There was no time to be afraid; Christy stepped closer and grasped its beak. It felt at once fragile and dangerous, as if she had put her hand around a folded cut-throat razor. With her free hand she tore at the netting, urgency overriding any possibility of untangling the bird with gentleness. The head had emerged from beneath the coat and the lidless eye reflected her flailing movements with no shadow of fear clouding its glass yellow. Suddenly the netting sagged; the heron was free. Christy heaved it towards herself, straining beneath the weight and the awkward mass of sharp bones, and staggered back into open water.

'Here, Maisie, take it,' she panted, finding a last burst of strength to pass the struggling creature up to her sister.

Cream silk smeared grey and tore as Maisie gathered the heron in her arms, its reed legs flailing pond weed across her skirt. In Maisie's no longer immaculate embrace the bird looked damaged and dangerous, stretched as tall as Maisie when it raised its beak, pulling her clamped hand up and around, stronger than she was although its neck was more slender than her arm.

'Quick, help me, I don't think I can hold on much longer.'

Christy scrambled out of the lake and they carried it together up to the house, Maisie supporting the neck and head, Christy bent over the body. They set it down in the wood-shed and waited by the door, watching in silence. Fluffing its feathers until they puffed like dough, the heron shook itself and began preening, the beak folding deep into down as it worked.

'I think it's all right,' Christy whispered to Maisie. 'Let's leave it in here for a while to make sure and go and get clean.'

In the house Frank had made a pot of tea, his morning ritual of the newspaper and ten o'clock toast and marmalade spread over the kitchen table.

Christy opened the door.

'Dad, something horrible has happened. The herons have slaughtered half the fish.'

Frank's tea slopped across the gingham tablecloth; he slammed out of the room and went out to survey the damage in the pen. Maisie and Christy had changed by the time he returned, and they led him out to the wood-shed to show him the surviving heron.

'They've done a hell of a lot of damage. We've lost quite a bit of money this morning.' Frank walked between his daughters, scarcely taller than Maisie who was dressed in too short trousers and a pink jersey that had belonged to Jessica.

The dispersal of Jessica's possessions was haphazard, and Frank was glad to see Maisie in her mother's sweater. She would keep it, wear it, wash it, until the scent of Jessica lingering in the wool distilled into the scent of Maisie. He had done no formal distribution of his wife's clothes and jewels; it was too final and painful to make a decision to be rid of the outer layers that made her real now that she wasn't. Easier and more appropriate to have them borrowed or asked for and to know that they would be used instead of remaining for ever in mothballs.

He and Christy had unpacked Jessica's belongings when

they moved to the farm, folding the clothes into her chest of drawers, the jewellery placed in her dressing table, her favourite chair and her mirror all grouped in the spare bedroom which he had painted pale blue like her bedroom in Lynton. He was aware that he was making a shrine of sorts but none of the children objected; Christy had even washed and ironed the lace curtains Jessica had loved and hung them at the window, tied back with yellow ribbons as they had always been. His own room was bare, underfurnished because there was nothing to put in it; all the bedroom furniture had been so feminine, so much Jessica's that he had hardly belonged in their room in Lynton. Christy made him some tartan curtains, Maisie gave him a bedspread for Christmas the first year they were at the farm, and Danny supplied his old lamp decorated with a trio of footballers in the Arsenal strip. The room was colourful and it held no poignant memories. It was fine.

He could see the tartan curtains dancing through the open window as he and the girls walked around the house to the wood-shed. They opened the door and stood a moment, their eyes adjusting to brown shadows within.

Christy saw the bird first.

'Oh no.' Her voice sharp, shocked.

In front of timber stacked neat to the roof, lay the heron, beak open, limbs still, yellow eyes closed.

Maisie put her arm around Christy.

'Never mind, at least it's not in pain. It would have been terrible to have released it and for it to starve to death.'

'But if we had left it alone it might have been all right.' Two tears rolled down Christy's face, then two more. She was surprised by how much she minded.

Frank carried the bird out and laid it in the yard.

'Probably shock,' he said. 'I can't say I'm not glad, even

though you did a great job getting it out of the lake. If it had lived it would have done the same again some time. Now we've got no herons living here, or not until the word spreads and some more come to prey on the fish.' He took Christy's hand. 'It's best this way. I would have had to shoot it if it was damaged, you know. And even though they're a menace, I love them.'

She forced herself to smile.

'I know, I know, and it killed my fish, so I shouldn't feel sorry for it, but I do.'

Maisie had wandered off and returned with two spades.

'Come on, let's bury it. I want to get on with my wedding plans.'

Frank's face froze in horror, and Christy laughed.

'You two can dig the grave then. I'm going to clear the pen.'

October sun, late to rise and slow to penetrate the earth after the bone-cold night, had dispersed the early mist from over the lake and shone a spill of copper across the unbroken surface. On the bank ducks and moorhens dozed, neat as curling stones on ice with their heads lost among their feathers. Christy fancied she could taste the smell of wet grass warming and yellowed leaves sinking closer to the earth as they rotted. She sat down on the jetty raising her face to the sun, putting off for as long as possible the moment when she had to collect the dead. Above her leaves whispered a roof of sound beyond which there was nothing. Her world ended with the lake now; Mick had ceased to be in her every thought when he dropped her off from London a week ago with a smile that flickered no further than his jaw. She hadn't seen him or spoken to him since. Nothing was resolved, but the balance had shifted and she had lost her faith in him. Maisie and Ben were getting married. Mick and Christy were splitting up. She could leave him now. She was independent and powerful. The fountain pen, tucked away in her underwear drawer, had a new significance. It could be her parting gift.

She pulled herself up and stood on the jetty, tall when no one was next to her, tall and braver than she had ever thought she could be. Braver than her mother had been. She had never faced the mess she made of Charlie's life, let alone Frank's life. Christy felt that by leaving Mick she was laying the ghost of her mother's restless soul. She had loved Mick, but she knew it was over. Jessica had died because she couldn't face her love affair being over. Christy was confident that she was not making that mistake. She would tell Mick on his birthday.

She rubbed her eyes, pushed back her hair and grasped the handle of the landing net, bracing her legs as she scooped under the surface and up around a cluster of bleeding trout. The plastic dustbin at her side was three-quarters full when she raked in the dead heron and laid it on top of the fish. Its neck twisted like silver rope, slack and useless but menacing, the final victim still hooked on its beak. Christy gripped both ends of the limp fish and slid it off the beak, shuddering at the tiny sucking noise of the wound as it closed around air. She held it up, opened its mouth and put her finger in to feel pink sandpaper teeth. She stroked the scales down smooth towards the tail then rasping as she ran her hand back up against the grain. It weighed less than a pound, not much more than a mug of tea, and its whole existence had been futile. Christy kissed the fish, more out of curiosity at the sensation than as a dramatic gesture, and dropped it into the bin. She had finished. More than seventy fish lay dead beneath the heron, and there were probably others that would die and float to the surface over the next few days. Frank would enjoy an evening wielding his calculator and would predict a lean Christmas as a result of this massacre.

Christy wiped her hands on the grass and walked back up to the house. She found her father with his head in his hands at the kitchen table amidst a chaos of lists and instructions in Maisie's firm handwriting.

'She says she's going to do it in May and I have to pay for it.' He sighed deeply and leant back in his chair. 'Her mother would be able to stop her. It isn't right, it simply isn't right. Why can't they carry on as they are?' He piled the papers up and pushed them into a drawer in the kitchen table.

Christy leant down over him, draping her arms around his shoulders.

'She might change her mind, Dad. May is a long way off and Ben's never here. Maybe she'll meet someone else.'

'You're right. I suppose there are decent people around in Lynton; after all, you found Mick. Perhaps she'll meet one of his friends. I don't care who she meets or what she does as long as she doesn't get married for a while. She's too young, she's got to live a bit.'

Christy turned away from him, her mouth dry and aching with the effort of keeping her expression bland. She put a bowl of cold cauliflower cheese into the microwave, laying the table for the two of them as the dish inside the oven rolled slowly to its climax and was stopped with a ping.

Frank glared at the squat oven.

'She can have that damn thing as a wedding present. I can't think why I ever bought it, it makes everything taste of Tupperware.'

Christy rolled her eyes and didn't answer.

Frank was only deflected from his dolour by the crisis of the dead fish. Heavy sighs accompanied the drum of

171

his fingers on the keys of the calculator and at half-past two he announced that things were not as bad as he had expected.

'But don't tell Maisie or she'll add another fifty people on to her reception list.'

Christy looked at the lists Maisie had made. There was one headed 'Outfits' with subtitles of 'Bride', 'Bridesmaids' and 'Father'. Her name was in the bridesmaid section; it was typical of Maisie not to have asked her if she wanted to be a bridesmaid nor to have mentioned anything about it before arriving with her plans laid. She noticed she was to wear a short silver dress and white tights. The whole notion of Maisie getting married was absurd to Christy. Her sister had never discussed it with her, nor indeed displayed anything but disdain and irritation in her dealings with Ben. Christy perused the lists for a few minutes, laughing out loud at the food one where Maisie had allowed her fantasy free rein and wished to have an ice sculpture carved of herself hand in hand with Ben, and stuffed them back in the drawer. She walked down to the office to meet the book-keeper, a sense of empty loneliness nudging through the mental list of her afternoon duties. At least Maisie knew what she wanted and she had plans. Christy only knew what she didn't want.

10

Hallowe'en and Mick's birthday arrived, the fourth Hallowe'en since Jessica had told her family she was dying. Christy liked the neat dovetailing of the dates. Mick had been busy since they returned from London and Christy had not wanted to see him before his birthday. She still half wanted to be with him; she missed him already. But she was resolved. Danny said he would come back for the weekend to see Mick on his birthday. Christy had given up the idea of a party: it wouldn't be appropriate.

She drove to the cottage in the early afternoon on Hallowe'en. Mick wasn't there, but the fire was lit in the sitting room and the kettle had just boiled. He appeared a moment later with Hotspur wet and muddy trotting behind him.

'Have you been gardening?' Christy smiled, glancing at the spade he was carrying. 'I didn't know you had green fingers.'

He grinned and kissed her.

'I wish I did, I'd love to tend a garden, you know.'

It was easy seeing him. Christy had spent too much time thinking of him as a cheap second-hand car dealer, a social-security fraudster. He had skulked in her mind, his eyes darting rat-like, glinting at a chance to make a few pounds. But here he was glowing as the warmth of the fire met flesh chilled from his digging, his face open, hugging her, telling her over and over, 'I'm so pleased to see you, sweetheart.'

The fountain pen was a parting present, but Christy couldn't bear to say so. She had spent hours doodling on the envelope of her card, wondering what to write, how to say 'It's over' and make it sound like 'Happy Birthday'. In the end she wrote 'Remember Me'. It looked like a tombstone inscription, but once she had fixed on it there was nothing left in her head to say.

Mick hardly noticed. He tore open the silver paper and opened the box clumsily, like a child in his excitement.

'Hey, girl, this is the best.' He held the pen up to the light, turning it, opening it, drawing the nib across his palm. 'And I was thinking you'd be giving me a razor in this little box.' He threw the box on to the fire. 'I don't need that, I'll be keeping it with me always.' He tucked the pen into the pocket of his shirt. 'Thank you, sweetheart, I've never had such a thing. My handwriting can't live up to it.'

He was holding her tight in his arms, pressing her ribs so the breath squeezed out of her and she had to push him away. 'Careful, Mick, you're squashing me.' They could talk later; it was a shame to spoil his birthday.

They went for a walk, holding hands through the woods, taking the straightest path because the glimpses of sky between the trees were pink and copper as if the sunset had started already. They came out on the other side, blinking at the melting horizon. It was late afternoon now and clouds were pressing down on the sun, forcing deep shadow in patches. Christy looked around very slowly, absorbing the strange selective brightness of the light.

Mick ran up a bank to photograph a row of poplar trees, their leaves burnished above black trunks.

'This is wild,' he shouted. 'I've not seen light like this anywhere.'

A scrawling line of geese bowled past out of formation on the back of the wind, the leaders dipped in gold, those behind fleeting silhouettes. Christy and Mick watched them wheel and turn along invisible air currents, skimming in and out of colour as the sun slewed beams across the fields. They turned back towards the cottage, walking faster as the pink behind them dulled.

'What a sunset,' said Christy. 'A real fanfare to mark your birthday.' She turned to Mick, but he was straining his eyes towards the cottage.

'Someone's turned the lights on. What do you make of that?' They ran up the track and in.

It was Danny. Sitting at the table carving chainsaw teeth on to a pumpkin.

'Hi there, I thought I'd come and say Happy Birthday, Mick,' he said. 'It's good to be back from that dump at last.' He started telling Mick about college and Christy went through to the kitchen to put the kettle on.

She'd left the cake in the car so Mick wouldn't see it, but it was dusk now. She went to get it before it was too dark to find the car. She had almost not bothered making one but it had seemed wrong to celebrate any birthday without a cake. It was an ambitious cake and she had gone to a lot of trouble with the illustration. She had made it in the shape of a folded newspaper, giving the surface over to an icing photograph and a headline: 'MICK FLEET HOOKS HIS FORTUNE'. The photograph had been very difficult to do. In the end she cut out a real photograph of Mick and stuck a red polythene fish across it. She had found the fish in a gift shop. It was Chinese and its packaging said it was a Fortune Fish. If you laid it flat on your palm it curled up to reveal your character. When Christy tried it, her hands powdered white with icing sugar, both sides of the little body curled up and in. 'This position represents fickleness,' pronounced the leaflet . . . She hoped Mick wouldn't try it out on her.

In the dusk she rested the cake on the bonnet of the car to add the candles and was about to go back in when she heard a car engine. I wonder who that can be, she mused, turning to look up the track. A column of headlights was approaching. Christy gasped, wondering if Mick had arranged a party. She remained where she was, rooted in astonishment, holding her cake. The cars spread in front of the cottage in a line and stopped, cutting their engines. As if a switch had been pulled they all flicked their headlights to full beam. Tiny red dots like predators' eyes appeared next to the cars, blue flashed above the glare and Christy stood in a flood of light, her hair a dazzling halo against the brick of the cottage. She screamed.

The red lights separated from the rest and bobbed towards her at shoulder-height and her throat closed in terror as she saw that they were attached to guns. Suddenly there were men everywhere, looming out of the cars, running towards her, pushing past into the cottage, crashing into the woods. Radios beeped and bled trailing voices into the darkness behind the cars.

A woman in uniform had her hand on Christy's shoulder. 'You'd better come with me, love.'

Still holding the cake, Christy followed her to a car.

'What's happened? I don't know what's going on. Why are there guns? Is it Danny?'

Dry-eyed and numb, she slid into the back seat of the car,

wedging the cake between herself and the policewoman. Maybe Danny had been arrested because of those bikers. They must have been drug dealers. Oh God, what if he was shot by a policeman.

'My brother, what are they doing with my brother?' She started to shake.

Danny and Mick were thrust out of the cottage door, their shadows dancing on the men behind them. Mick was handcuffed. Danny was not. She leapt out of the car and ran over to them.

'Keep out of the way, miss.' The policeman behind Mick raised an arm to stop her touching him. Danny pulled her away.

'It's OK, Chris. Come with me to the police station and we'll get this all sorted out.'

'What's going on? Please tell me.'

Christy's numb shock gave way in sobs. She rubbed at her eyes, frantic to stop herself crying. She looked round for Mick, but he was already in a car. She saw the doors shut; she saw him taken away. She turned back to the policewoman.

'Do I have to come with you or can Danny and I drive ourselves?'

'You can drive yourselves, love. No one is arresting you.'

Christy headed back to the cottage to get her bag, but the woman stopped her.

'Sorry, miss, you can't go in. The house is being searched.'

Christy glared.

'This is crazy, I just want my handbag. What are they looking for anyway? I need to go and get my things and I'll have to take the dog as well. Perhaps you could go in for me.'

The policewoman nodded.

'Just wait there, please, and I'll see what I can do.'

Christy and Danny waited. The cottage was alive with disruption. Black-clad men swarmed through the small rooms, past the windows, staggering beneath heaps of books and papers. The lights were on everywhere and all the doors were open.

'Danny, tell me, please tell me what's happening. Why have they got Mick? Are you all right?'

Danny hugged her.

'I don't know. I'm scared, Christy. I don't know what's happening. But it's big. Look at those guns.'

His arms around her were light and thin; she hugged him back, half of her exhilarated with relief that none of this was to do with him.

'We need to find the dog.' Christy broke away and ran around to the back of the cottage.

She whistled, praying Hotspur hadn't run off. He crept towards her from the wood, his head low, crouching in apology.

'Good boy, come on, Hotspur.' Soothing him calmed Christy.

She walked back towards the car where Danny waited, her mind clear as comprehension settled. She felt no surprise. This was always going to happen; she realised it now. Mick had lied again when he said he was a car dealer and had stolen a cheque. The truth was something worse by far. 'Oh God,' she whispered and crouched to pick Hotspur up.

Danny drove to Lynton, Christy with Hotspur shivering on her lap sat next to him. They followed the police convoy with Danny talking all the way. He had grown up in a sudden spurt; he was in control now.

Christy sighed.

'I left my cake in the police car,' she said, and started laughing, silly with shock.

Danny squeezed her hand. 'Calm down, it'll be OK. We'll find out what's happened at the police station.' Danny leant forwards over the steering wheel, his face illuminated by the police car lights in front. 'This is crazy, isn't it?' He laughed nervously, his eyes round and wild staring at the road.

Christy lit a cigarette. She couldn't tell Danny her thoughts, he admired Mick so much.

'I thought they had come for you,' she said.

The car jerked with Danny's surprise.

'What do you mean? Why?'

Christy was worn out and close to tears; she sighed again.

'Oh I thought you'd got involved in drugs or something. I don't know, but it was Mick anyway.'

Danny looked across at her.

'What do you think he's done?' he asked carefully. 'You don't know, do you?' He sounded so worried, frightened that Christy might be involved in this nightmare of guns and handcuffs and sirens.

'No, I don't know,' she said. How could Mick have done this to them? He had told so many lies. Rage took over from Christy's shock. 'I'm leaving him anyway,' she said. 'And it's not because of what's happened today.'

Lynton's yellow night glow seeped into the car as the convoy reached the outskirts. They were approaching the police station.

Danny said quickly, 'I think we'll have to give statements to the police. I wonder if we'll be allowed to see him?'

'I don't think we will,' said Christy. 'But we'll be able to visit him later on.'

Danny slowed the car in front of the police station.

'Maybe they'll let him out. It might be a mistake.'

Christy's head ached, otherwise she was numb.

'It isn't a mistake. There will be a trial.' She opened her window and dangled her hand in the fresh air.

The convoy, with Mick somewhere in its midst, snaked around the building and in through an iron gate. Danny parked on the road, inching back and forth to make sure he was not on a yellow line. Christy pushed Hotspur over into the back.

'I'll see him through the trial. But it's over. I was going to tell him that tonight; I'm glad I didn't. But after the verdict, that's it.'

Danny grinned at her.

'What if he's found innocent?'

'He can have his dog back,' said Christy. She got out of the car and followed her brother into the police station.

The day of the verdict was hot. As I drove to court, clouds puffed high and hung weightless in the blue morning. I saw two magpies and a black cat. 'Two for joy, two for joy,' I chanted under my breath as I joined the queue of people snaking into the court house. Mick's case always drew big crowds; in the last days the security-searching took as long as a weekend supermarket check-out. Nausea made me tremble and to forget it I smoked, leaning against a pillar, staring up at the sky. I wondered what Mick had been given for breakfast today. Surely they would have made an effort on the final day of his trial. I imagined cooking him breakfast tomorrow. At home. In another life. I would make scrambled eggs, the china would match and Mick would read the paper while I poured coffee. A plush cat would roll its pink tongue through a saucer of milk accompanied by the murmer of the radio. I might wear an apron.

'Here, Christy love, you come this way.' A policewoman beckoned me through a side door. 'I can search you here and get you up to Court 4 before the hordes. That way you'll be sure of a seat.' She frisked me as she spoke, patting my pockets and running a metal detector over me with the brisk gentleness of a mother preparing her child for school.

I wore my red linen dress for the verdict. It was short. The second metal detector, the one right outside Court 4, went wild and the skinny policewoman waving it glowed peony pink when I wriggled out of my bra without undoing my dress. I could have just told her it was my underwear, but I was so nervous I thought I had to take it off.

'Now try. I think it was the clasp on this, or its under-carriage, or whatever they call it.' I stuffed the bra in my handbag and she whisked me through to the courtroom.

The public gallery was already full. The hordes had beaten me. None of the court staff were in yet. They would swarm a second or two before the Judge arrived and just after Mick came up from the cells below. I slammed out of the door again into a crowd of people already waiting for seats to come free.

'There's no room in there.' I banged my fist on the desk in front of the little policewoman. 'I can't go in to see the verdict.'

She bobbed nervously, as if she was curtseying to me.

'There must be a mistake, I'll just check.' She vanished into the courtroom and a moment later was back herding a vast woman with a face pockmarked like a pincushion. 'I'm sorry, Christy.' The policewoman was on tiptoe whispering in my ear so the furious pincushion couldn't hear. 'This one slipped past me. I had saved you a place, now in you go.'

I slid into my seat between two old men and crossed my legs, tugging the hem of my dress down, horribly conscious of the bareness of my thighs. Mick and his attendants took their places in the dock. I blew him a traitor's kiss and he tried to smile. He was wearing the shirt I had bought him as a good-luck present; the price tag dangled behind his shoulder and made me think of evacuated children during the war. I shivered, feeling stupid and angry as I realised for the first time that none of his family had come over for the trial. Maybe they didn't even know about it.

The clerk who was fussing around with his papers stood to attention as the black flock of barristers and solicitors entered.

'Rise in court,' he then commanded and the Judge swept in.

The jury had still been out at the end of the session the day before, but this morning, following a night in a hotel, they had reached a verdict on all four charges.

In his summing up the Judge had sent them out to

182

deliberate with the words, 'Members of the jury, you must look at the evidence and reach your verdict upon that evidence. You must decide beyond reasonable doubt whether or not Mr Fleet is guilty as charged. Remember, Beyond Reasonable Doubt.' It seemed such a feeble phrase upon which to hang a future.

They filed in and sat down in their familiar formation. Everyone was looking at them, trying to gauge their expressions and see inside their minds. I glanced along the public gallery, wishing Dad was with me. He would be waiting outside with Maisie. Danny was back at college again until Maisie's wedding.

The Judge spoke.

'Members of the jury, have you reached your verdict on all four charges?'

The foreman rose, formal in a tweed suit and probably very hot.

'We have, Your Honour.'

In the dock a navy-blue wall of policemen merged behind Mick. His head was bowed, he was no longer tall. His eyes hooked like claws on the jury. None of them returned his gaze or glanced at me. They didn't even turn to the Judge but stared into glassy space.

'The first charge. Do you find the defendant guilty or not guilty?'

'Not guilty,' said the foreman.

Until that moment a shell so fine I hadn't known it encased me had been protecting me from reality. I sank as it cracked open and strength welled out of it.

'Second charge. Do you find the defendant guilty or not guilty?'

'Guilty.'

I couldn't remember what the second charge was. There

183

were two bank robberies, one burglary and a possession of firearms charge but I had long ago lost track of which order they came in.

'Third charge. Do you find the defendant guilty or not guilty?'

'Guilty.'

I forced myself to look up. The two ladies on the jury whom Mick had won round were crying. Lemon Face pressed a handkerchief to her mouth and the man with the Roman nose had his fists knotted as if in passionate prayer.

'Fourth charge. Do you find the defendant guilty or not guilty?'

'Guilty.'

Mick had not moved. He was stone-faced and staring as if in a trance and his scar was livid and pulsing. He still looked the same, he still was the same, but he was nothing to do with me now.

I cried and cried as Tobin and the Judge talked about weapons and former behaviour. It would have been better if I had left him when he was arrested. Now my treachery was greater; he would always think I had left him for his guilt.

The Judge scribbled a few notes and speaking slowly, as if he were dictating to a new secretary, pronounced the sentence.

'Because of the serious nature of the crimes committed and to ensure the safety of the public, a custodial sentence is in order.'

Blood drummed in my head. Mick was going to prison. I longed for a cigarette.

'Fifteen years . . . eighteen years . . . ten years to run concurrently . . .' The Judge powered on, throwing Mick's life away almost randomly. 'Take the prisoner down now,

184

please.' The tone in which he requested this was mild and anti-climactic.

I thought I was screaming, but it must have been in my head because Mick went away without looking at me.

A Note on the Author

Born in 1964, Raffaella Barker is the author of *Come and Tell Me Some Lies*. She lives in Norfolk with her husband and two sons.